MW01125812

LUSAM

THE DRAGON MAGE WARS

BOOK ONE

by

DEAN CADMAN ©2015

www.deancadman.com

First published 2014
This edition published 2016 by Dean Cadman
ISBN-13: 978-1523280919
Copyright © Dean Cadman 2015

Visit www.deancadman.com to read more about the
authors publications and purchase other books by the author.
You will also find features, author interviews and news about
forthcoming books and events. Sign up to the mailing list so
that you're always first to hear about any new releases.

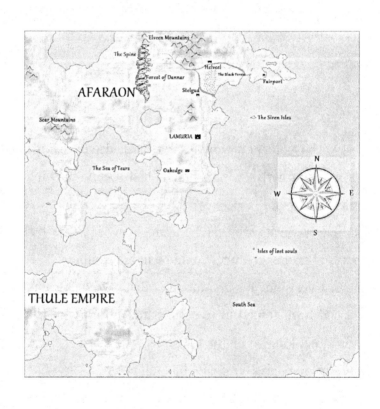

Chapter One

The cold rain came down hard, driven by the strong northerly wind which had been blowing relentlessly for the past three days. Winter was definitely on its way, and Lusam knew it. If he did not find shelter soon he would be in big trouble.

Ever since his grandmother died two years ago, he had been forced to live the hard, unforgiving life of a street kid. Living on the streets was hard enough, but for a twelve-year-old boy alone in a city like Helveel, where thieves and murderers were commonplace, it bordered on the impossible.

Lusam spent the first two years after his grandmother had passed away living in the alley behind the baker's shop. For the most part, he only had to compete with the rats for scraps of burned or spoiled food thrown out by the baker or his wife. The dead end alley also helped him shelter from the wind, and although meagre, the baker's chimney gave off a small amount of heat, especially first thing in the morning when the ovens were lit to cook the daily bread. In fact, the only reason he had found the alley, which had undoubtedly saved his life that first year with its bitter cold winter, was that chimney.

Almost starving, he had smelled the bread cooking from the chimney and it had led him to that alley. Lusam found a small grate in the wall that first day, and had managed to crawl inside it, out of the worst of the cold. There wasn't much room to move inside, but at least it was dry, and the small space helped retain a portion of his body heat. He didn't need a lot of room as it happened. Apart from his well-worn clothes, his only other possession was a small crystal amulet his grandmother had given him the day she had died. She had told him that his mother had entrusted it to her for safe-keeping, and that she should give Lusam the amulet when he came of age. Lusam had tried to ask about the amulet and his mother, who he never really knew, but his grandmother was far too ill from the fever to be able to answer any of his questions. He had fully intended to ask her more in the morning, after she had rested, but he never had the opportunity, as she quietly passed away in her sleep that very night.

Lusam had thought many times about selling the amulet to buy a little food, or even one night's warmth at an inn, but no matter how much he told himself he needed to sell it, he couldn't bring himself to part with it. It was the only thing he had left of his mother and grandmother in this world, and selling it for any reason seemed so wrong. So this small insignificant hole behind the baker's shop became his home and safe retreat from the night-time city for almost two years.

One morning, stirring from his sleep, Lusam noticed an unusual smell. It was nothing like the mouth-watering smell of freshly baked bread to which he would normally awaken. At first he thought it part of the dream he was having; it's funny how the mind can take real sounds and smells, and incorporate them into your dreams, making them all the more real. He was very comfortable this morning. An almost spring-like warmth surrounded him in his small living space, the likes of which he had not felt in months. He started drifting off, back into deeper sleep, dreaming of the summer evenings spent with his grandmother in the forest, cooking food over an open campfire with the stars overhead twinkling down on them.

His grandmother had once told him that one of those stars was his mother watching over him while he slept each night, and that had given him great comfort in the cold, dark, lonely nights since he had found himself all alone in the world. As he was drifting deeper into sleep, he was startled awake by a cry of: "Help! ... Fire! ... Fire!"

When he opened his eyes, he could not believe what he was seeing. The bakery was engulfed by flames, with thick black smoke billowing out of the windows and under the door. The flames leapt through the roof and high into the morning sky. As he started to take in the scene more, and his mind started to process the information through the haze of sleep, he noticed the heat inside his small grate increasing rapidly. He quickly removed the grill from the entrance and was about to poke his head out to take a better look, when a large piece of burning timber landed directly in front of his face, bouncing twice down the alley before coming to rest in a shower of sparks. He knew he had to get out of there fast, before the rest of the building came down on top of him. With a silent prayer to Aysha, that no more of the building would come down on him while he was climbing out, he took a deep breath and wriggled out of the hole as fast as he could.

When he was able to stand, he began to run as fast as he could towards the far end of the alley, away from the burning buildings. From behind him came a huge crash. As he looked back over his shoulder, he saw that the front of the building adjoining the bakery had collapsed right where he had been only seconds before, burying his grate entrance in a mass of rubble and flames. As he stood watching the carnage unfold before his eyes, the cold realisation suddenly hit him. He had lost yet another home.

No matter how poor a home it had been, at least it had been his, and had kept him dry. Then a second thought struck him with even more force. He had just lost his main food source too.

He had no idea how long he stood there staring dumbfounded at the flames, while people were trying to contain the fire and save what they could, and the rats ran in all directions, fleeing for their lives. When Lusam finally regained some of his composure, he simply turned around and walked away from the relative safety of the alley, and into the unforgiving streets of Helveel.

Two weeks had passed since the fire, and Lusam had spent most of that time cold, hungry and tired. He sat on the edge of the fountain in the main square, listening to the water behind him cascading down a statue of some long dead king. He watched the people walk past for hours, all busy in their own little worlds, never taking any notice of the street kid sitting on the small wall of the fountain watching them go by.

He had hoped that the baker's shop would be repaired, and that he could go back to how it had been for the last two years, but the damage had been far too severe, and it had been pulled down instead. Life was much harder now. There were plenty of street kids in Helveel, but there was also a distinct hierarchy among them. Although Lusam had been in Helveel for the past two years, he had not associated himself with the street kids there much, so they didn't know him, and therefore, he was a long way down the pecking order when it came to anything, especially food or work.

Many of the street kids had to resort to theft on a daily basis simply to survive. If caught they would be severely punished with a public whipping for their first offence, and having a digit removed from their hand for any future crimes they committed. Many of the street kids had various numbers of digits missing: it seemed the older they were, the more they had lost. It was simply a choice—steal or starve.

Lusam refused to resort to stealing anything. This was not because he was frightened of the consequences, although he didn't relish the thought of either type of punishment. When he had been a young boy his grandmother had caught him taking a freshly baked biscuit without permission from the window sill, where they had been left cooling. She had been most vocal in her displeasure with him. Although, obviously he never got whipped or lost a digit over the biscuit, he also never forgot the lesson she had taught him, that stealing was wrong in any form, and he had given his word to her that he would never steal anything ever again.

While he sat there in the weak winter sunshine, he couldn't help but think about all the good things he used to enjoy doing with his grandmother. His favourite was when she would take him into the forest and teach him small tricks, like how to light a camp fire with only a word, or how he could communicate with the animals. He remembered the time he asked her if they could talk back, but she explained that she wasn't really talking to them, she was simply projecting a feeling towards them. She could make a bird, or a rabbit come right up to them by projecting a feeling of safety towards the animal. He practised for hours until he could also do it. In fact, he got so good at it, he could summon several different creatures at the same time with little effort.

He had used a similar method in the alley to keep away the rats at night. He would project the image of a hungry cat as if it was waiting behind the grate, ready for a tasty rat supper, and it seemed to have worked very well indeed. He did feel a little guilty about doing this sometimes, because he once asked his grandmother why she didn't just get the animals to come to them, and catch them for their dinner, so they would always have meat for the table. She looked him straight in the eyes, and with that stern look she used to wear whenever she wanted him to know something was important, she had replied: "*You should never betray the trust an animal gives you willingly, or unwillingly. To use the power Aysha has given you in that way would dishonour her and yourself in equal measure, and that would not be wise in many ways, my child."*

She had also explained that all life had a force of magic running through and around it, and even some things that were not alive had a certain amount of magic within them. Each person had an amount of magic inside them, most could neither sense it nor use it, but a gifted few could see it in others, and even fewer could use the power inside themselves to varying degrees.

She taught Lusam to recognize the aura that glowed around everyone, and how he would notice it glow more intensely around the few who could use magic, and to be very wary of such people if he did not know them.

One of his favourite games as a young boy that he had played with his grandmother, was hide and seek in the forest. When they first played the game, he could never understand how his grandmother was able to find his hiding places so easily. When it was his turn to seek, sometimes it would take what seemed like forever to a young boy to find her, and many times he called out that he *"gave up,"* and that she should come out of hiding.

On one occasion when they went to the forest and played the game, he had the idea of looking for his grandmother's aura instead of looking directly for her. He was amazed when he cleared his mind, concentrated, and searched using his mage-sight—instead of his natural-sight—that he could spot her so easily, and from so far away, even through the trees. He soon realised how she had won the games so quickly in the past.

He was about to suggest they did something different, as it would be far too easy to find each other now that he knew her secret, but then he had an idea. With a mischievous grin on his face, he told his grandmother he would go and hide, and not knowing he had discovered her secret, she readily agreed and started counting to the mandatory one hundred. Lusam ran a few hundred paces into the forest, just as he had done dozens of times before during his previous visits. He found a suitable hiding place, and crouched down behind a large fallen tree. He closed his eyes, cleared his mind as he had been shown countless times, and he tried to hide his aura using magic. He had no idea if it would, or even could work, but he had to try, then maybe he could win for once.

He could see his grandmother stand up from her starting point and head directly for his hiding place using her mage-sight. `No!` he thought to himself, and redoubled his efforts to hide his aura. It was a strange feeling he experienced, like a shutter had been lowered over the lantern that was his mind. He knew the light was still as bright behind the shutter, but no light escaped to the outside world. He saw his grandmother halt in mid-stride, and then start to look around frantically in all directions. He knew for certain at that point he had achieved his goal, and smiled to himself, knowing he was at last going to win for a change.

His grandmother stood still for a few more seconds, before resuming her original line of interception. He was pretty sure she couldn't see his aura, so he presumed that she must be just heading towards the last place she'd seen him. He was just about ready to accept defeat again, when he had another idea.

He concentrated on projecting his aura to a location about fifty paces to the east. He then set the image in his mind and released a short, sharp blast of power in that direction. Instantly his grandmother turned to look to the east, and then changed her direction to where he had projected his fake aura.

Lusam by this time was chuckling to himself so hard he was surprised his grandmother didn't just hear him instead of see him. When she reached the place he had projected his aura she stopped, then started scanning the ground all around her. Even at fifty paces he could see the worry and concern on her face as she started calling out his name.

Rules were rules, and the rule was if you didn't say the words, `I give up,` you didn't reveal your location, or you lost, and at the age of seven rules were very important; almost as important as winning the game.

After a few more minutes his grandmother must have also remembered the rules because she called out the correct phrase, indicating that Lusam had won the game and should come out of hiding. He did just that with a very loud "*Whoop!*" while jumping into the air, over and over again. He also noticed the relief that washed over his grandmother's face when he emerged from his hiding place as she rushed over to hug him tightly.

"I won, I won, I actually won this time!"

"Yes, you did indeed. Come, let's go sit by the fire, I need to talk with you Lusam."

Lusam felt a little apprehensive as they headed the short distance back to their camp. He wondered if he was in big trouble for playing the trick on his grandmother. When they reached the camp and sat down, his grandmother sat there for what seemed like a very long time just looking at Lusam, then eventually she said in a calm voice, "Lusam, how did you do that? How did you hide your aura from me?"

"I'm sorry, I didn't mean to make you angry with me. I won't do it again. I promise," he replied sheepishly.

"No, you don't understand Lusam. What you

just did is supposed to be impossible to achieve, and to my knowledge, I have never heard of it ever being done before. Could you do it again, here, now for me please?" she asked him. He looked up at her and nodded his head. "Thank you Lusam," she replied, watching his aura closely.

He cleared his thoughts again and closed the shutter in his mind just as he had done before. This time it was much easier, because he knew exactly what he needed to do to achieve it. His grandmother brought her hand to her mouth, gasping out loud, and a small tear rolled down her cheek, dripping onto the back of her quivering hand.

"Are you alright grandmother?" he asked, suddenly concerned.

"Oh, yes Lusam. I'm more than alright my boy," she replied with a huge smile on her face.

Later that evening she asked him in more detail how he had done it, and she tried for a long time to hide her own aura with his help, but she was unable to do it, or even come close.

One of the most vivid memories of his early

years that had stayed with him right up until now, were of that day in the forest. The simple things like winning a game, or being able to do something an adult couldn't do. One conversation however stuck in his mind more than any other from that afternoon around the campfire.

His grandmother took hold of his hand and looked deep into his eyes, then said, "Lusam, I thank Aysha, for you have been doubly blessed. Not only can you use the power Aysha has granted you, but you can also now hide amongst the non-magi of this world."

He looked at her while his seven-year-old mind tried to process what she had just said. "Hide? Why do I need to hide?"

"Oh, my boy, there is a lot of this world I must teach you. The lessons here in the forest you have learned well, surpassing anything I could have imagined. Many things I must teach you must wait until you are older, so you will understand them fully. I must ask something of you now, so it may help ensure that we *do* have the time we will need for me to teach you all that I must. Promise me, that you will use your new found skill and shield your aura at all times. If possible, even while you sleep. Can you promise me this Lusam?"

"But, why grandmother?"

"Please Lusam, if you love me, you must promise me you will do it. For me, and for you." He looked at his grandmother's pleading expression and knew he had to agree, even if he didn't know the reasons why.

"I'll do it for you, don't worry grandmother."

"Thank you Lusam. It means so much for me to hear you say that," she said, taking a hold of him in her arms, and hugging him so hard he could barely breathe. It was a good feeling, and he missed those times so much now he was older, and all alone in the world.

Thinking about all the good times he had as a child was all well and good, but it did little to relieve the discomfort coming from his stomach, as it loudly reminded him he had yet to eat anything today.

Lusam had already been to the main gate earlier

that morning. It was the place where all the street kids gathered each day, and where they all tried to gain some kind of work, for food or coin. Sometimes a rich nobleman may simply need information regarding the whereabouts of a certain building, or person. Or it could be something as disgusting as clearing out a blocked sewer pipe, or some other equally degrading job that nobody else in town wanted to do. All the people of Helveel knew that the street kids gathered at the gate each morning, desperate for anything they could get, and so they knew exactly where to find the people to do the jobs that nobody else wanted to do in Helveel.

It was a long-shot, but he stood up and headed back down to the city gates. Nobody would usually try to find street kids there at this time in the afternoon, because they knew they wouldn't be there. If the work didn't come in the early mornings, it didn't come at all, and the kids would have to try and eat by other less reputable means.

As he approached the gates he noticed a pretty blonde girl about his own age already standing at the gate. Although her clothes were dirty, they were cleaner and in much better condition than his own attire. She wore green trousers and a brown tunic with sturdy looking black boots, and her shoulder length hair was neatly tied up in a pony tail. He had seen her the previous morning at the gate, but she had kept to herself, and not really spoken with any of the other street kids waiting for work there. As he approached she made brief eye contact with him, and when he nodded his head in greeting, she did the same in return.

"Hi there … are you waiting for work, or are you just meeting someone here?" he asked in his friendliest voice.

"Why do you ask?" she replied, with more than a hint of caution evident in her voice.

"Sorry, I was just trying to be polite. I didn't want to take any job you might be waiting for," Lusam said smiling.

The girl stared at him for a moment, trying to decide if he was making fun of her or not, then after a brief hesitation she said, "There aren't many polite people around these parts. Being polite means you usually go hungry."

"That may be so, but I was taught that manners don't cost anything. Nothing can be lost by using them, but much can be gained," he said smiling at her, pleased with himself that he had remembered one of his grandmother's teachings so well.

She looked directly at him, raised an eyebrow and said, "And what, exactly, do you think you will gain from me?"

His face instantly flushed with embarrassment, as he realised how she had mistaken the meaning of his words.

"No … no … I, I didn't mean it like that at all," he stammered, feeling his face grow even redder, if that was even possible. The girl started to smile, and when she could no longer hold back her amusement, she burst out laughing, pointing at his beaming red face.

"You should see your face, it's a real picture! It's redder than the knights' tabards."

Lusam didn't know whether to laugh or cry

with embarrassment, but he settled on the former, and they both had a good laugh at his expense. Eventually, when they both calmed down enough, Lusam offered a hand towards her.

"My name's Lusam."

"Neala. Pleased to meet you Lusam," she said, still wearing a huge smile. "Are you new here? I haven't seen you around here much."

"No, actually I've been here in Helveel for about two years now since my grandmother died, but until recently I … I had other accommodations." He didn't think that telling Neala he had lived inside a grate, and had eaten mostly stale bread for the past two years would impress her very much, so he decided to skip those details entirely.

After talking together for about an hour, it turned out Neala herself was quite new to Helveel, and had only just arrived there a month earlier. She had lived in the southern city of Stelgad, which she described as being even worse than Helveel for its crime and filth, which he found very hard to believe possible. She told him of her life there, as part of a thieves' guild in the city, and how she had been taught to defend herself through the tutelage of her guild master, and others in her guild.

Neala had been, until recently, quite happy with her life in Stelgad. That was until a rival guild ambushed them, and killed most of her guild members in a swift and deadly surprise attack. Apparently, Neala had only managed to escape the massacre through sheer luck. The night it happened, she had been on an errand to fetch more wine for one of the guild member's birthday celebrations. She recounted the obviously painful memories of that night to Lusam. She told him that as she was returning with the wine, she could see a huge fire in the distance, and soon discovered it to be her own guild headquarters that were fully ablaze. She had tried to get closer and see what was happening, but fortunately she had noticed the men on the ground, and on the rooftops above, all dressed in the dark brown cloaks of a rival guild. As her own guild members tried to flee the burning building, they were shot down mercilessly by the crossbowmen on the rooftops opposite. They had no chance of surviving, nor would the rival guild allow any to survive, as was the way of these things. No survivors, meant no one to claim future revenge.

Having witnessed the destruction of her entire guild with her own eyes, she knew she must leave the city immediately, or the enemy guild would find and kill her too. If she left right now under the cover of darkness, they would most likely assume she had perished in the fire along with so many others of her guild.

Neala knew exactly which businesses in the city were owned by the enemy guild, and decided to steal a horse from one of them. It wasn't much revenge for what they had just done to her friends, but at least she would cost them a horse, if nothing else.

Neala had spent the next ten days on the road surviving as best she could, until finally arriving at Helveel, where she sold the horse, and then tried to blend in while she decided what to do next.

One of the local thieves' guilds she'd approached had refused to hire her, claiming they weren't hiring any new members at the moment, but Neala knew better. The guilds were always hiring new members, simply because they lost so many members to enemy guilds, and the law keepers. Neala knew that the real reason they wouldn't hire her, was simply because they didn't know her. They feared that she might be a spy from a rival guild trying to gain entry into their organisation. The big problem for her now was, that after she had approached that guild and being refused entry, it was entirely foolish to try a second guild. She would almost certainly be under close observation now by several of the original guild members, just in case she actually was a spy, and tried to report back to any rival guild. If she even went near another guild now, the order would be to kill her, and she knew it. Her only option left in Helveel, was to live as she was at present, on the streets, and wait until other, better opportunities presented themselves.

Daylight was rapidly turning to dusk when they agreed to walk back towards the town square together. The street traders would soon be packing up for the day, and the small roadside cafes would be preparing for their evening trade yet to come. Lusam had often found that it was worth being around the stalls as they packed up. On several occasions Lusam had been asked to help pack up stalls, and had been paid a coin or two for his troubles. On more than one occasion he had found a coin on the floor, hiding between the cobbles as the stalls were being dismantled. The coins must have been dropped by a careless patron or trader at some point earlier in the day. There was also occasionally spoiled food left by the vendors, either by accident or intentionally, he couldn't be certain.

As Lusam and Neala started to walk up the cobbled street towards the town square, they saw a finely dressed man approaching from up ahead. When he was within hailing distance he called out, "Hey! I need one of you kids for a job. I need this letter delivering across town with the utmost urgency," he said, brandishing a small folded brown piece of paper with an address written on the front, and a wax seal placed upon it. The address on the letter read:

T. Zachery,
The Apothecary,
West Helveel.

Glancing at the letter in the man's hand Lusam said, "Sir, I know where the apothecary is in west Helveel, I can show this girl where to deliver it if you'd like."

The man looked very shocked at Lusam's statement and said, "How can you possibly know where this letter is destined to be delivered young man?"

"I'm sorry, I just glanced at the address on the front of your letter. I didn't mean to pry into your business sir, please forgive my rudeness," he said, bowing his head slightly.

"Are you trying to tell me that you can read boy?" the man asked, with an almost comical look of disbelief on his face. The only people who could usually read and write were the high-born, the clergy or the scholars of this world. For a street kid to be able to read and write was unheard of, but Lusam had been taught from a young age by his grandmother, along with many other useful things.

"Yes sir. I can read and write," Lusam replied beaming with pride.

"Show me your hands boy," the man said pointing towards Lusam. Lusam tentatively showed the man his hands, wondering to himself why he would be interested in his hands at all.

"Well I never … A street kid who can read and write, and has all his fingers, whatever next!" the man exclaimed, shaking his head slightly.

"The payment is two silver. One now, and one upon me receiving the reply from Mr Zachery. Do you understand?"

"Yes sir," they both said at the same time.

"Good. Bring back his reply as soon as he gives it you. I will be waiting for you at my shop in the east district. It's called `The Old Inkwell.` Just ask anyone for directions in the east quarter, and they will point you in the right direction if you don't already know the place." The man handed Lusam one silver coin, gave him one last dubious look, then turned on his heels and headed back towards the town square.

"Here's your money," Lusam said, offering the silver coin to Neala. "I'll show you where the shop is. Come, let's hurry, it will be dark soon. It's not good to be in that part of town when the sun goes down."

"Thanks, but you keep the coin. The man said he would give us two silver for the delivery, that's one each by my reckoning. Although I could be wrong, I'm obviously not the smart one here," she said with a mischievous grin on her face.

"Oh, you don't have to give me your money. You were first in line for the next job that came along. It doesn't really seem fair if take your money," he said, feeling his cheeks flush red again. "And I'm sure you're much smarter than me anyway," he added, grinning right back at her.

"There you go again, with those lofty ideals of yours. I've told you once already at the gate, they'll only make you hungry," she said, still smiling at him. "Besides, when you arrived at the gate I was about to call it a day anyway. So, if you hadn't come by to lecture me with your high and mighty morals, I would have missed the job anyway, so it's only fair that we split the money," Neala replied, trying very hard to keep a straight face. Lusam stared at her for a few seconds before realising she was teasing him again, and they both burst into fits laughter, playfully nudging each other as they set off walking in the direction of the apothecary.

Chapter Two

Although the sun had not yet passed the horizon, it was still much darker in the narrow streets of the west district. The tall houses loomed overhead blocking out what little daylight there was left, as they cast their long shadows onto the street below. As they began walking down the damp cobbled street in the shadows of the houses, Lusam began to realise why the man had offered to pay two silver coins so readily, for what had seemed like such an easy job at the time. During the day these streets were much like any other in Helveel, but at night they were not for the faint-hearted. There were numerous brothels and seedy bars in this part of town, all setting up for the evening trade to come.

Nobody walking past them so much as looked at them, let alone gave them any form of greeting. This part of town even smelled different, like a combination of rotting vegetation and old beer, with a strong smell of sewage mixed in for good measure.

As they passed through a short tunnel under a large warehouse complex, known locally as The Arches, Lusam became aware of footsteps coming from behind them. He glanced back over his shoulder, but couldn't make out anyone lurking in the shadows behind them. He turned towards Neala and began to inform her in a whispered voice that he thought someone was following them. Neala turned her head towards Lusam and gave him a slight nod, letting him know that she already knew, then just carried on walking as if nothing was wrong.

Lusam wasn't sure if Neala had understood correctly. Maybe she had nodded her head in answer to some other unspoken question, and didn't actually know about their pursuer lurking in the shadows not too far behind them. Nervously, he leaned towards her and whispered, "I think someone is following us back there."

"I know!" Neala hissed back at him, sounding a little annoyed. "Keep walking, and stay quiet."

They both increased their speed and rounded the next corner, only to come face to face with a filthy looking man holding a knife out menacingly towards them. When he smiled, he showed a mouth of missing and half rotten teeth. He had a vicious looking scar running down the left side of his face, from just under his eye, to the corner of his mouth.

Leering towards them he spat to the side, then in a rasping voice he said, "G' me your money, or I'll gut ya both here and now!"

Neala took a small step towards the man and calmly said, "Do we look like we have money to you?" All the time staring the man straight in the eyes. "I suggest you put the knife away, before you get hurt."

Lusam couldn't believe what she was doing, he slowly put a hand on her shoulder to try and make her see sense before either of them got hurt by this man. Neala just turned and winked casually at him, then returned her steady gaze back to the man.

The man looked almost as shocked by her response as Lusam was. Then he started laughing, spat to the side again, and then said with a mocking tone in his voice, "And who's going to hurt me little girl, you? I warned you to pay up or else. Now …"

Before he could finish his sentence Lusam noticed something flash in Neala's hands, it was so fast, it was barely visible. The man fell in a crumpled heap on the floor clutching at his throat, as he bled out on the cobbled street.

"I warned you too," Neala said to the man on the floor in front of her, now lying in a pool of his own blood. Dead. Standing there in complete shock, Lusam almost didn't hear the running footsteps behind him until it was too late. As he turned, he saw a huge man flying through the air at him, brandishing what looked like a meat cleaver. Without thinking, and on pure instinct, he released a huge blast of power towards his assailant. It literally stopped the man in mid-air, and blasted him back down the cobbled street, sending him crashing into the wall of

The Arches. He hit the wall with such a sickening crunch it curled Lusam's toes, and the man sank to the floor, never to move again. He didn't need to go and see the results of what he had just done, he simply knew that nobody could have survived that kind of impact.

Lusam and Neala stood there looking at each other with equal measures of shock and awe on their faces.

"Let's get out of here, before anyone else comes. The last thing we need is the town guard being called," Neala said in a hushed voice. As they quickly walked away from the scene, Neala turned to Lusam and said, "What the hell was that you did back there?"

"I could ask the same question of you," replied Lusam defensively.

"I've already told you that I grew up as part of a thieves' guild in Stelgad. You didn't think they taught me to do needle-work there do you?" she spat back him. "I don't remember however, having the conversation where you told me you were some kind of powerful sorcerer though!" she hissed at him.

"That's because I'm not a sorcerer. I've no idea how I even did that back there. I just panicked, and the next thing I knew he was flying backwards into that wall," Lusam said, trying to match the brisk pace Neala was now setting. "When I was younger, my grandmother taught me a few bits of magic, but nothing like that!" Lusam said in a hushed voice.

"Oh … just like that, she taught you, `some magic tricks`. You say that like it's the most natural thing in the world Lusam. Magic is supposed to be only myth or legend Lusam, not something your grandmother teaches you! We need to talk about this later. Here isn't the place. Let's just get this job done, and go get paid," she said looking at him warily.

"Yeah, good idea," he replied, as they both hurried to leave behind the shadier part of west Helveel.

As they approached the apothecary, they noticed a man leaving the shop and begin locking the door.

"Looks like we're just in time," Lusam said, nodding towards the man.

"Yeah, looks that way," Neala agreed.

When they got closer to the man, Lusam called out to him, "Excuse me sir. Are you Mr Zachery?"

The man turned his head to look at them approaching, and after taking in their shabby appearance replied suspiciously, "That depends who's asking, and for what reason young man?"

Lusam smiled at the man in an attempt to get him to relax, but it seemed to have the opposite effect.

"Sorry sir. My name is Lusam, and this is Neala. We have a letter to deliver to a Mr T. Zachery from the owner of The Old Inkwell. We were instructed to bring it here to the apothecary in west Helveel, and to take any reply back to him," Lusam replied in the most official voice he could muster.

"In that case you're in luck, I am Thomas Zachery, the owner of this establishment," he replied, gesturing towards the shop behind him. "Please, hand me the letter, and I'll see about that reply young man."

"Thank you sir," Lusam said, handing him the sealed brown letter.

The man opened the letter and started to read the contents. After a short time he looked up at Lusam and said, "Please inform Mr Daffer that I will have the items he has requested delivered to his premises in the morning by ten o'clock, and thank him for his patronage. If there is nothing else, I would bid you both good evening, and I'll be on my way home now. My wife will surely be waiting for me to arrive for the evening meal, and she gets more than a little upset if I keep her waiting." Mr Zachery nodded his goodbye, then he turned and started walking away from them in the opposite direction.

"Must be nice to have a meal waiting for you at home," Neala said quietly in a wistful voice.

"Must be nice to have a home," Lusam replied in a similar manner.

"Yeah, that too," she agreed.

"Come on, let's go back and get paid, then maybe we can go eat something too. I'm starving," suggested Lusam.

"Sounds good to me. But, can we go back a different way from the way we came? By now it's a good bet the town guard will have been called, and it's probably best to avoid them if possible, just in case anyone saw us there and gave them a description of us," Neala said, looking a little worried.

"I'd love to avoid that area, but unfortunately, if we try to go back through the northern quarter at this time of day we'd be arrested by the town guard for sure. Anyone who's not from the higher classes found in the northern quarter after dark is immediately suspected of criminal behaviour, and as we only have a verbal reply from Mr Zachery, we wouldn't have any proof of why, and where we were heading. As much as I hate to admit it, it's still our safest way back to the town square, and then onto the east quarter," Lusam replied, with an apologetic look on his face.

"Sounds like we better avoid going through the northern quarter then," Neala agreed. "But, if we intend going back the way we came, we had better get going, before the place is crawling with guards."

They turned and started to retrace their path

back towards the town square, through the dark cobbled back streets of west Helveel. Just before they rounded the corner of the area where the earlier attack had occurred, they stopped dead in their tracks, and listened intently. In the distance they could clearly hear the approaching sound of marching boots on the hard cobbles. A unit of the town guard was approaching their location, and they seemed to be coming up the cobbled streets behind them; the sounds echoing off the houses of the built up narrow street.

"Quick, let's get moving!" whispered Neala, as she quickened her pace towards the bend in the road, with Lusam trying to keep up with her. Acting on instinct, she glanced around the corner before making herself visible to anyone that might be waiting there. She saw a small group of guards already at the grisly scene inspecting the bodies. Neala grabbed Lusam by his shirt and quickly pulled him out of sight against the wall.

"What's the matter?" he asked quietly.

"Guards. Lots of Guards. We're trapped

between them," she replied in a hushed voice. As they stood there trying to decide what they should do, out of the corner of her eye Neala noticed the a patrol appearing from the direction they had just come. Without a second thought she grabbed Lusam around his neck, pulled him close to her, and started kissing him. "At least try to look like you're enjoying yourself," she whispered in his ear.

All Lusam could do was nod his head and give a very sheepish reply of, "Hmm Hmm," before Neala once again covered his lips with her own. The guards marched straight past them and around the corner, without a word to either of them. Lusam's heart was beating faster than he could ever remember it doing before in his entire life. He wasn't sure if it was the close call with the guards, or the shock of what Neala was doing to him.

As the last guard disappeared around the corner and out of sight Neala broke off the kiss, and with a sigh of relief said under her breath, "That was too close." Lusam just nodded at her with his mouth open, and a dumbstruck look on his face. Although he would never have admitted it to Neala, that was the first kiss he had ever had from a girl—and a pretty girl too.

"It's okay, you can close your mouth now," she said, with a huge grin on her face. "Well, I didn't think it was possible to make your face any redder than it was at the gate earlier, but obviously I was wrong about that," she said, trying hard not to laugh at his expense. "Come on, let's get out of here. Take my hand, then let's walk past them as if we're only lovers out for a stroll. Just remember to keep smiling a lot and you'll be fine," she said, still grinning from ear to ear.

"Yeah, okay," was all he could manage. And off they walked hand in hand as if nothing else in the world mattered, gazing into each others' eyes, as they casually walked by the guards. Lusam was acutely aware of the guards taking notice of them as they walked past, but none of them approached or asked them to stop, so they carried on walking, ignoring the guards completely. As they approached The Arches where the big man's body still lay, Lusam became aware of a man kneeling down inspecting the body. He was wearing a long black robe, black shiny boots, and had a gold chain with a symbol of some kind hanging around his neck. His skin was much darker than the average person, and it reminded Lusam of tanned leather. Although his appearance was strange enough, it wasn't the shade of his skin, or the richness of his clothing that caught Lusam's attention most. It was the aura that surrounded the man. Not a delicate blue aura like everyone he had ever seen before, but an intense crimson aura that shone out like a bright moon in a pitch black sky.

"Keep walking," Neala hissed in his ear, while pulling at his hand.

Lusam hadn't even realised he had stopped walking, and with a quick glance at Neala, he resumed walking towards the strange man and the body. When they came within a hundred paces, the man stood up and turned to look directly at Lusam and Neala. Fear suddenly flooded Lusam's mind. He could feel the strange man trying to gain access into his mind, and so he instinctively tried to stop him

45

from entering. He could feel his defences being probed for weakness from all angles, but when Lusam realised that the man couldn't break through his defences, he visibly relaxed. Lusam had a few moments to think before they would pass by the man. He remembered back to the game of hide and seek he'd played in the forest with his grandmother, and decided to try and distract the man in the same way. He focussed on a place further down the cobbled street, around the corner from where they had just come, and let his magic flow, projecting his aura towards that location. It instantly had the desired effect. The strange man seemed to lose all interest in them. At first, he began walking very swiftly towards Lusam and Neala, but he didn't even slow down as he walked straight past them, heading directly towards the point where Lusam had just projected his aura.

As they walked towards where the body still lay slumped against the wall, Lusam wondered what the strange man could have been looking at so intently. Apart from the dead body, he couldn't see anything else there to hold the man's attention so long. That was until he used his mage-sight to take a look, and then he couldn't believe what he was seeing. The whole area around the body pulsed with power, and even the wall where the man had impacted glowed a soft blue. It was like a thousand blue fireflies hovering all around the area.

"Incredible," he whispered.

"What is?" Neala asked.

"Oh, nothing. I'll tell you later. Come on, let's get out of here," he replied, not particularly wanting to start a conversation right at that moment. As they passed back under The Arches, Lusam tentatively glanced back one last time, but to his great relief he could see no sign of the strange man with the intense crimson aura following them, and so, they headed back to collect their hard-earned coin from Mr Daffer at the Old Ink Well in the east quarter.

When they eventually arrived at the Old Ink Well, they were relieved to see a light still coming from a ground floor window. That light meant Mr Daffer was still at his shop waiting for them, and that in turn meant they would most likely get paid for the less than straight forward evening's work they had just undertaken. Lusam knocked on the door three times, and then waited for an answer. He was just about to knock a second time, when the door opened and Mr Daffer stuck out his head. He looked both ways up and down the street, and then gestured for them to quickly enter the shop, which they did.

The shop was much larger on the inside than it looked from the street outside. The building stretched a long way back, and had dozens of bookshelves lining the walls, with all kinds and sizes of books. Lusam had never seen so many books. In fact, he never imagined there could even be so many books in the world, let alone in one shop in Helveel.

After they had both entered the shop, Mr Daffer quickly checked up and down the street once more, before closing the door and turning to speak with them.

"So, did you deliver my letter boy?" he asked, looking directly at Lusam.

"Yes, we did sir. Mr Zachery said he would

deliver what you requested before ten o'clock in the morning directly to your shop, and thanked you for your patronage," Lusam replied.

"Good. Good. A job well done then. Here is the other silver coin I promised you," he said, handing the coin to Lusam.

"Thank you sir. If you need any further work doing in the future, we would be very happy to do it for you," Lusam said, maybe a little too enthusiastically.

"I'll bear that in mind boy," he replied with a thoughtful look on his face.

"Actually, there is a job I might need help with. I recently inherited this shop from a relative of mine, and I have discovered a rather large store room downstairs in the basement full of books. I require them sorting out into categories, and the titles recording. It's obviously a job for someone who can read and write like yourself. Call by here tomorrow at noon if you are interested in the position. There should be fewer people in the street at that time of day to see you enter my shop dressed as you are. I also need time to think of an appropriate amount of money to pay you for the job, as well as the best way to achieve the fastest results," he said matter-of-factly.

"That sounds like something we could do for you no problem sir," Lusam said with a smile.

"I don't need both of you. I only need one, and as you're the only one who can read, that would be you boy," he said, with an irritated tone in his voice.

Lusam knew he was definitely in the minority when it came to reading and writing in Helveel. The fact Mr Daffer would have to pay a scholar many times the amount he would have to pay Lusam, gave him a certain amount of leverage, and that's even if he could find a scholar willing to do such a menial task. He stood there a few moments longer, then decided to take a gamble.

"We're a team sir, Neala and I. We could do the job much faster together, than I could by myself," Lusam replied, not feeling half as confident inside as he just sounded out loud. Neala visibly shifted her stance. She too was surprised at what he had just said, but to her credit, she held her tongue and stayed silent.

"Is that so boy?" Mr Daffer said, raising one eyebrow at Lusam. The silence seemed to stretch on and on as he paced back and forth across the floor of his shop. To Lusam's great relief it seemed that Mr Daffer finally came to the same conclusion a short time later, when he turned to him and said, "You can both work together, but the pay is for one person only. I will pay you three silver a day, which you will have to share if you want the job."

Lusam looked at Neala and she nodded her agreement to him.

"We agree to your terms. Thank you sir," Lusam said in a slightly shaky voice, and offered his hand to Mr Daffer, who took it in return.

"Oh, and one other thing. Stop calling me "sir." My name is Tom, or Mr Daffer if you prefer," he said with a slight smile.

"Sorry sir ... I mean Mr Daffer," stuttered Lusam.

"Just make sure you're back here tomorrow at

noon, and ready to work," he said, shaking his head slightly.

"We will, and thanks again," Lusam called out, as they left the shop and closed the door behind them.

With a huge smile of satisfaction on his face, Lusam started to make his way back towards the town square, with Neala at his side. A few moments later, Neala suddenly stepped out in front of him, making him stop dead in his tracks.

"Why did you do that back there?" she asked, with a strange look on her face.

"Do what?" replied Lusam innocently.

"You know full well what I'm talking about. You could easily have lost that job by demanding I *had* to help you. That was a damn foolish thing to do!" she said, staring straight at him. Then she surprised him even more, when she kissed him on the cheek.

"Thank you Lusam. That was very kind of you, nobody has ever done anything like that for me before," she said smiling at him, just before playfully punching his arm.

"Now come on, let's go eat, I'm starving!" she said, as she started running towards the town square, with Lusam trying hard to catch up with her.

***

For almost a year now Renn had secretly followed this disciple of the dark god Aamon. Renn was hoping that he would lead him to the boy-mage known as Lusam, who had been lost over two years before when his guardian, Asima, suddenly grew ill and died. His guardian sent reports only once every year to the High Temple of Aysha, to reduce any chance it may be intercepted by the agents of Aamon. The reports would never contain anything as foolish as a name or description of the boy, or the location he was staying. Only the bare-essential information required by the High Priest to judge his progress were included in the report, and even that was written in an ancient secret code only known by a select few of the followers of Aysha.

It was only when the death of a minor mage

was felt by the High Priest, and the report that was due failed to arrive, that concern grew rapidly for the welfare of Lusam. Renn and the High Temple were certain he was not dead. If he had died his passing would also have been felt by the High Priest and other servants of Aysha.

Whenever a mage-child is born into the world, a great pulse is felt within the fabric of magic that surrounds all living things, by all those capable of sensing magic, both good and evil. The only thing stronger than this, is the much larger disturbance felt when a mage departs this life.

Asima agreed to serve Lusam's mother Samara as *Hermingild*, or more commonly referred to as *The all giving*. Asima, during her lifetime had been a fairly weak mage only capable of minor magic, but she had been well-schooled in all its forms at the High Temple. In her declining years she willingly agreed to accept the great honour and responsibility of becoming *Hermingild*.

Asima had only one task as *Hermingild*, and that was to sacrifice herself at the exact point when a mage-child was born. When the sacrifice happened, the larger pulse from the death of the *Hermingild* would be sufficient to mask the birth of the new mage. If done correctly the followers of the dark god Aamon would not become aware of a new mage being born, only seeing the death of a mage instead.

This practice had only become necessary around two hundred years ago, when it was discovered that the Kingdom of Thule to the south had been secretly, and systematically killing all the newborn magi they could find. It was first discovered that they had a hidden network of agents in the land of Afaraon, whose sole job it was to secretly kill any newborn magi in the land. It had long been known that a birth or death created a ripple effect in the fabric of magic. What wasn't known until around two hundred years ago, was how the agents of Aamon managed to find the location of the births so quickly, and accurately.

It was at this time that the order known as the *Paladins of Aysha* were used to combat the ever increasing threat to the total eradication of magic in the lands of Afaraon. Nobody knew exactly how many centuries the killing of newborn magi had taken place in Afaraon, but one thing was certain, around two hundred years ago the agents of Aamon became very good at their evil task.

Magic was almost wiped out in the lands of Afaraon, with no new magi to take the place of the old as they died of natural causes and old age. It was at this time the practice of *Hermingild* was started by those first brave old magi, to give magic a chance to survive in the lands of Afaraon.

Soon after, it was discovered how the agents of Aamon were able to determine the location of the births so easily. It was discovered they each wore a magic ring capable of communicating with each other over great distances. Whenever a birth occurs it creates a ripple outwards from the birthplace, just like throwing a stone into a pond. With the agents in constant contact with one another they sense the ripples hit them at slightly different times, and can calculate the area of the birth very accurately, also learning which one of them is closest, and therefore he or she becomes the assassin.

On the day of Lusam's birth his *Hermingild* arrived just in time, and fully intended to perform her duty, but unknown to Samara or Asima fate had other ideas. As Asima carefully prepared herself for the birth and her own ultimate sacrifice, custom dictated she must examine the mother magically to determine the precise time of delivery. Being just a moment or two early, or late would result in her sacrifice failing to have the desired effect, and the discovery of the newborn mage by their enemies. As she examined Samara she discovered that she was not having a single baby as expected, but instead twins. Even more alarming was the fact that one of the babies was struggling badly to survive, even before the birth. She suddenly realised if she sacrificed herself on the birth of the first child as planned, when the second child was born, its birth would be felt by the agents of Aamon, and they would still track down the mother and newborn within a short time, and kill them both. The agents searching for the baby would soon discover that two babies had actually been born, and maybe also discover the secrets of the *Hermingild* at the same time, and that simply could not be allowed to happen.

Asima used her limited power to examine both babies in minute detail whilst still in the womb, and what she found startled her. The first baby was not formed correctly, and could not survive more than a few moments after birth, but the second baby was in good health. If they were born in the correct order, the birth of the healthy baby would be felt by the agents of Aamon, closely followed by the death ripples of the second baby. If this happened Asima would not have to sacrifice herself, and could serve another mother as *Hermingild*, further helping magic to prevail in the land of Afaraon.

The problem was that the unhealthy baby was already engaged in the birthing position. She would have to reverse this and engage the healthy baby instead, using her magic, and the midwifery skills she had learnt at the High Temple. Asima quickly explained the situation to Samara, who by this time was in a great deal of pain from the labour, and sweating profusely. Samara agreed there was no other way and asked Asima to begin the procedure of repositioning the babies, but first she must do something for her. Samara reached up and took an amulet from around her neck, clutching it tightly until the latest contraction pain subsided. When it finally passed, and while gasping for breath, she concentrated hard and cast an amazingly complex spell on the amulet, creating a eerie glow upon it as she did so. Asima had no idea what the spell had done, and there was no time to ask for explanations at this point.

Samara then grabbed hold of Asima's hand, placed the amulet in her palm, and made her swear she would give the amulet to her surviving child when he or she came of age. The old woman looked into the eyes of Samara and swore she would, but insisted she would be able to give the child the amulet herself after all this was over. Samara just smiled and gently shook her head, then insisted Asima proceed before it was too late.

The repositioning of the babies was a long and

incredibly painful experience for Samara. Asima was worried she would not be able to endure the procedure, and that further complications would ensue from an unconscious mother, making what they had planned impossible to achieve in the time frame allowed. Amazingly, and to her credit Samara stayed conscious, and the first child was born without further complications. The second baby however was far from straight forward, and refused to be born.

Time was running out fast. By now the agents of Aamon would have sensed the birth and be well on their way. The second baby must be born before they arrived to achieve the deception they required, and before it died naturally in the womb. Asima tried to think frantically of an alternative solution, but could not come up with one that would work in the time they had left.

Samara, gritting her teeth through the pain reached over and took hold of her hand, then reached into her belt and removed her dagger, before giving it to Asima. Placing the dagger in her hand, and clasping it with both of her own, she looked straight at the old woman and nodded silently. Asima knew exactly what she wanted her to do to save the new baby, and as hard as she tried she could not think of an alternative to the grisly, but only option now available to her. She bent forward and kissed Samara on the forehead. Then smiling at her with tears in her eyes, sadly nodded her reply. Asima placed her hand on the mother's forehead, and spoke the words of a basic spell that would put Samara to sleep while she carried out what was necessary.

Moments later the second baby was free of his mother, and as expected only survived a few breaths, before peacefully passing away whilst lying against his mother's body. Asima felt the pulse of magic flow through her as the baby took his final breath, and was equally sure the agents of Aamon had also felt it. The old woman did not posses the skill to heal Samara of her wounds, even if there had been enough time to attempt it. Taking one last look back, with tears freely rolling down her cheeks, she clutched at the baby swathed in a blanket, and prayed silently to Aysha for Samara's soul. Then she turned and disappeared into the woods with the newborn child.

All of this information was contained in the first report sent from Asima to the High Temple. At that time it was decided that she would raise him as her own kin, under the guise of being his grandmother. She would be responsible for his safety and early training, and then when he came of age deliver him to the temple for his more advanced training to begin. That was almost fifteen years ago now, and somehow Lusam was still alive, possibly within this very city, and it was Renn's job to find him.

***

From within the shadows Renn looked out of the warehouse window, and down onto the cobbled street below. The agent of Aamon was kneeling down inspecting the body of a middle aged man whose throat had obviously been cut. The agent had been eating a simple meal at an inn four streets away, when he suddenly stood up and left without finishing his meal. Renn had secretly followed him to this location, and after seeing the two bodies from a distance, one of which displayed the unmistakable residual effects of magic being used on it, had decided to find a vantage point in one of the warehouses above the scene. Here he stood, carefully watching the agent of Aamon from within the shadows.

He suspected this man was probably a necromancer by the black full length robe he wore, and the gold chain that held the symbol of his god Aamon hanging loosely around his neck, but he had not yet seen him perform any magic to be completely sure. When Renn had first arrived and looked out from the warehouse window, he had noticed a group of five town guards inspecting the bodies. The agent had briefly spoken to the five guards, and now they were casually talking amongst themselves, seemingly unaware of the two bodies that lay in the street. As Renn watched the agent kneeling beside the first corpse, he noticed a small amount of magic being used, but he couldn't determine exactly what the effect had been.

After several minutes the agent stood up,

walked over to the second corpse, and knelt down beside it, just as he had done with the first. He seemed much more interested in this corpse however, as Renn would have expected. If Renn could see the residual magic that had been used, then it was certain the agent of Aamon would also be able to see it.

Several more minutes passed before Renn noticed a boy and girl walking up the street towards the grisly scene. He saw the couple stop and lean into the wall for a kiss and cuddle. Renn instinctively scanned both of their auras for signs of magic, as he had done hundreds of times in the last year, but saw nothing of any significance. As he resumed watching the agent, he noticed another guard patrol entering the cobbled street heading their way. When the new guards met the first patrol they stopped and began talking among themselves. He noticed the two lovers resume walking towards him again holding each others hands, whilst giggling and laughing, as young people in love often do. Just as Renn momentarily went back to concentrating on the agent again, he was sure he sensed magic come from one of young couple, but it vanished as fast as it came. The agent stood up quickly and turned in the direction of the two lovers, who were now standing still looking at the corpse he was standing over. He could see the girl pulling at the boy's hand, eager to get away from the grisly scene. Renn checked their auras again to be certain, but he was sure neither lover were capable of using magic, and once again turned his attention back to the agent. From down the street, just out of sight, came the blinding flash of a powerful aura: someone down there was using magic.

The agent of Aamon walked quickly past the two lovers, and down the cobbled street in the direction of the magical disturbance both he and the agent had just witnessed. Renn knew he had to follow the agent, as he may lead him to the boy-mage. He was about to leave the warehouse and try to catch him up, when he saw the agent returning back up the street, this time at a much slower pace. Renn watched as the agent casually walked up to the group of guards. He spoke a few words of magic, waved his hand, and the guards formed up in rank. Renn then watched as they marched back down the street, towards where they had originally come from.

"Neat trick," Renn said quietly to himself.

Renn watched as the agent remained there for a moment longer with a thoughtful look on his face, then he appeared to momentarily glance directly up at the window where Renn was hiding. Renn moved further back into the shadows to make sure that he couldn't be seen. The agent then turned his attention back towards the corpse with the magical residue. He walked slowly over to the corpse, and confirming Renn's earlier suspicions, he began chanting a dark spell to raise the corpse from the dead. At first the corpse began to twitch a little. Then came a groaning noise from deep within its throat, and then finally, it began to try and stand up. Even from this distance Renn could hear the broken bones grinding and snapping as it struggled to stand before the agent of Aamon. When it finally managed to stand up, he could clearly hear the necromancer questioning his new minion.

"Can you understand me?" the agent asked in a

thick southern accent.

"Yesss massster," replied the huge corpse.

"Good. Now tell me, who killed you?"

"A boy killed me massster," the corpse hissed back.

"Would you recognize the boy's face again?" asked the necromancer.

"Oh ... Yeeesss massster."

"Good! I command you to find and kill this boy, and anyone else who gets in your way. Do you understand?" asked the necromancer, with an evil grin on his face.

"Yeeesss masster ... I shall obey," replied the undead corpse, before turning and slowly disappearing through the tunnel under the warehouse complex.

The necromancer watched, as his minion slowly walked away into the city in search of its new prey. The agent then turned and started walking back down the cobbled road again, in no apparent hurry to get anywhere fast.

Renn stood in the shadows a moment longer,

thinking about the two choices he now faced; he could continue to follow the necromancer, and lose track of the vile creature sent to kill the very person he had been sent to protect, or he could go kill the creature before it managed to complete its mission, and then try to find the necromancer at a later time.

It only took him a moment to decide: the vile undead creature had to die. Its very existence was an affront to both himself and his God, and it must be destroyed as soon as possible, before it could do anyone any harm. He left the warehouse building behind, and started to track down the undead creature. Killing it would be easy. Killing undead was exactly what paladins were born to do. All he had to do was find it, before it found Lusam.

Chapter Three

Lusam was sitting on the edge of the fountain waiting for Neala as the sun came up over the distant hills. They had both agreed to meet at the fountain early the next morning, while eating their well-earned meal the night before. Despite the troubling events of the day before, it had still been one of the best days Lusam could remember since arriving in Helveel. He knew he had made a good friend in Neala, and he felt sure she felt the same way about him. They had both also gained employment for at least the next few weeks, thanks to their new employer Mr Daffer at the Old Ink Well.

Lusam even had a few coppers left in his pocket from the previous night's meal. And so, he had decided to call at the new baker's shop on his way to the fountain, and buy two small freshly baked loaves of bread for their breakfast. There was nothing that tasted better first thing on a crisp, cold winter morning, than warm freshly baked bread, and he was hoping Neala would get there before it went cold.

"Morning," came the familiar voice of Neala. She walked around the fountain wearing her ever present smile, and sat down beside him on the wall.

"Good morning," he replied, smiling back at her, and handing her a packet of warm bread.

"Thanks Lusam. You're so sweet," she said kissing him on the cheek, which only made his smile grow even more.

They both started eating the warm bread and were almost done when Lusam asked, "What do you think we should do until noon? There's no point going to the gate for work today."

"No, I guess not," she agreed, taking another bite from the warm loaf.

"I was thinking maybe we could go out of town for a walk in the forest this morning. If we're lucky there might still be some huckleberry thickets, or even hackberry around that we could gather."

Neala laughed. "I wouldn't know what a huckleberry or hackberry looked like if it hit me between the eyes."

"It's okay, I can show you. When I was a boy, my grandmother used to take me into the forest, near where we used to live, and we would collect a whole basket full of them. They look like large wild blueberries, but taste really sweet. They should be very ripe at this time of year," he replied eagerly.

"Okay, okay, I give in. Lead the way master woodsman," she said with a grin, and an over enthusiastic attempt at a bow. Laughing and joking they both headed for the east gate of town, both knowing that was the most direct route to the forest outside of Helveel. When they passed the guards at the gate they were given no more than a cursory glance by either guard, and continued on their way unchallenged.

Twenty minutes later they crossed the small wooden footbridge that spanned the river, and arrived on the east bank next to the forest.

"Don't get us lost in there," Neala said nodding towards the forest.

Lusam laughed and replied, "Those woods aren't big enough to get lost in. Thirty minutes in any direction would see you back out of them again. Not like the forest in the Elveen mountains where my grandmother used to take me. If you got lost in there, you could have walked for days amongst those trees and never seen daylight."

"Sounds delightful," she said sarcastically.

"Tell you what, I'll hold your hand if it makes you feel any safer," he replied with a grin, using the same sarcastic tone she'd just used on him, and before they took another step, they both broke out in fits of laughter.

Sure enough Lusam was right, the huckleberry were in plentiful supply, and very ripe and sweet. Neala didn't like the taste of the hackberry, complaining they tasted too tart and she didn't like the seeds inside, but she seemed to like the huckleberry just fine. They spent a while gathering a few handfuls each, then found a clearing with a fallen log to sit down and eat them in the dappled sunlight filtering through the trees.

After a few minutes of quietly eating the berries Neala broke the silence and said, "I guess now would be as good a time as any to talk about what happened yesterday. How you managed to blast that big guy down the street into that wall the way you did?"

Lusam stopped eating and just looked at her, not really knowing what to say. "To be honest, like I said when it happened, I really don't know how I did it. I just heard running footsteps coming from behind me, I turned, and saw that huge guy flying through the air with a meat cleaver, ready to chop me into bits and I panicked. All I remember is wanting him as far away from me as possible. I put my hands up to protect myself, and the next thing I saw, was him flying backwards away from me into that wall," he replied in a calm even voice.

Looking directly at him, and after thinking for a while she replied, "Okay, let's say I believe you about that part, for now. What about the part where you told me your grandmother taught you how to do magic when you were a boy? Everyone I've ever met doesn't believe magic exists in the world anymore, and it's only something dreamed up by story tellers, or written about in ancient tales and the likes. Until yesterday I felt the same way, but I can't deny what I saw you do with my own eyes. So tell me what your *'magical grandmother'* taught you, or maybe better still, show me something, so I can better understand."

"Well, I really don't know what I could show you. She taught me how to light a fire with magic, but that hasn't done me much good in Helveel, because it's forbidden to light fires in town. She taught me how to talk to animals, which was quite useful for keeping the rats away at night, but other than that, the rest was only about mind preparation and concentration techniques. The rest of the time was spent with normal things like reading, writing and other stuff," he replied shrugging his shoulders.

Neala looked at him with disbelief written all over her face before saying, "Please don't make fun of me Lusam, now I know you're not telling me the

truth. Nobody can talk to animals. Not even you!"
She stood up ready to walk away, but Lusam put his
hand out and took hold of her hand.

"Wait. Please. Let me show you. Come sit
down and be still a minute," he said gently to her.
Neala paused a few seconds before doing as he asked.
She sat down next to him, fully expecting some
excuse to be forthcoming as to why he couldn't
perform this impossible task.

Lusam relaxed his mind, and then searched the
surrounding area for any wild animals using his
mage-sight. It wasn't long before he found a burrow
of rabbits and several birds only a short distance from
where they were sitting. Concentrating, he called to
the animals and birds with a combination of promises
of food and feelings of intense safety. One by one
they emerged from their hiding places, and
approached the fallen log where the two humans sat
side by side holding hands.

Neala's face was a real pleasure for Lusam to
behold. As she sat there in complete astonishment,
several birds landed on her legs and shoulders, and

four large rabbits came and sat by her feet, grazing on the vegetation right in front of her. Neala looked too scared to even move, just in case she startled the animals and they ran away, so she just sat there watching them intently, happy to simply share the space with them all.

"Sorry, I couldn't find any wild unicorns to summon for you. You will have to make do with rabbits and birds I'm afraid," he said, trying not to burst into laughter at the look on her face.

All Neala could manage was a single word. "Incredible!" she whispered, gripping his hand as if her life depended on it.

They sat there for maybe half an hour while Neala watched the animals—and Lusam watched Neala. Then remembering they had to be back by noon, he gently coaxed the animals away from them, before releasing them altogether. Lusam was about to suggest they should head back to town, when Neala threw her arms around his neck and gave him a huge hug.

"I'm sorry Lusam. I'm sorry for not believing

you. That was the most amazing thing I have ever seen. Thank you Lusam," she whispered in his ear.

"You're welcome," was all he could think of to say in reply. "We better head back to town. We don't want to be late on our first day."

"Yes, you're right, we better head back," she agreed smiling at him.

"Oh, and just so we're clear, I *was* joking about the unicorns, they don't really exist," he said in a serious voice, trying hard to keep a straight face.

"HA! HA! Very funny," she replied playfully smacking his arm, while still smiling from ear to ear. As they turned and started walking back towards town, Neala reached down and took hold of his hand, and all the way back to town constantly asked him questions about how he had spoken to the animals, and what other kinds of magic he could do. Lusam just smiled, happy being in Neala's company, and answered the best he knew how.

As they approached the street where Mr Daffer's shop was situated, Lusam looked up at the sun and judged the time to be as close to noon as made any difference, and so felt quite confident Mr Daffer would not think them late for their first day at work. Lusam remembered the first time they had come to the shop, when Mr Daffer had seemed overly concerned that someone would see them entering his establishment. At the time it seemed a little rude and confusing to Lusam as to why it should bother him so much if anyone saw them enter, but having had time to think about the situation from his point of view, it made more sense now. Given the fact that usually only the wealthy, clergy and scholars could read, it stood to reason they were his main clientele in Helveel. If that was the case, having a couple of dirty looking street kids be seen by any of them entering his shop would do his business no favours at all. With that in mind, Lusam suggested they wait until the street was clear before knocking on the door of the shop. Once the street was clear of people, they quickly approached the door and knocked loudly three times.

Mr Daffer swiftly opened the door, almost as if

he had been eagerly waiting on the other side for them to knock. He poked his head out of the door and quickly looked up and down the street again, before beckoning them inside the shop.

"Quickly. Quickly, please, in you come," he said in a hushed voice. Then he turned the sign over in the window so it read *'Closed,'* and locked the door behind them.

"Good day to you Mr Daffer," Lusam offered in his most polite voice.

"That remains to be seen young man, but at least you weren't late, so that's a good start I would say," he replied smiling.

Lusam noticed movement out of the corner of his eye, and as he turned he noticed a middle aged woman in a light blue dress standing up from behind the counter.

"I would like to introduce you both to my wife Lucy. Lucy, this is Lusam and Neala. They are the two I told you about who will be helping us catalogue the books in the basement."

"Nice to meet you both," Lucy replied, nodding

her head and smiling.

"Nice to meet you too," they both replied in unison.

Mr Daffer cleared his throat and said, "I think the first order of businesses today will be for us to lay down the ground rules here at *The Old Inkwell.* That way we won't have any misunderstandings between us while you are in my employment. If you disagree with any of them, or feel that you can not comply with them, you are free to leave any time you like. I hope that sounds fair to you both?"

"Yes, of course," replied Lusam, while Neala just nodded her head in agreement.

"Good. First thing you should know about *The Old Inkwell* is that although I have only recently inherited the business, which has in fact been running here in Helveel for well over two hundred years. We are a highly respected establishment, who cater for every kind of clientele, from the lowly student in history just starting out, to the master scholars of the high universities. One thing they all have in common however, is a high status in society, and as such are not inclined to conduct business in any establishment that is seen to employ dirty looking street kids. No insult intended."

"We had already thought about that as we approached your shop, so we waited until the street was clear before knocking on the door," replied Lusam, slightly defensively.

"I thank you both for your diligence. However, it will only be a matter of time before the inevitable happens and you are spotted entering or leaving, or possibly even come face to face with some High Lord inside the building itself. I can not take that chance, so I have taken the liberty of asking Lucy if she could dig out some of my son's old clothes that will fit you, as the ones you're wearing are little better than rags, and will never survive the washing process. As for you Neala, I'm afraid we never had a daughter, but I did notice your clothes were in much better condition the last time you were here, and only in need of a good wash. You can also wear some of my son's clothes until we get yours cleaned, if that is acceptable to you both?"

Lusam and Neala looked at each other, then both nodded their agreement to Mr Daffer without speaking.

"Good. Now that's settled. The next thing I wish to discuss is your current accommodations. Where are you currently sleeping each night?"

Lusam looked at Neala and replied, "Well, Mr Daffer, that depends, it can change from night to night."

"And it also depends what time of year it is," Neala added.

"Hmm … Just as I suspected. Neither of you have a permanent place of residence do you?"

Feeling slightly embarrassed by the question—which surprised him, as it really wasn't their fault they were on the streets—Lusam just shook his head, and Neala followed his example.

"I have already discussed this subject with my wife Lucy, and we both agree that, given the fact you may be in our employment for some time, we feel it would be best if you stayed here at *The Old Inkwell*. The location this building now occupies, was the exact spot where an ancient temple once stood. Although the building you now see is much newer, and obviously was built for a much different role, the old underground rooms and store rooms of the original temple were incorporated into the newer building, and so still remain. I'm sure we can adapt a couple of the old accommodation cells the monks used, and make them comfortable enough for your stay here. If nothing else, it will certainly be warmer and more comfortable than the streets I'm sure, and your clothing will have a much better chance of staying presentable at the same time."

Lusam certainly longed for some place to call home again, even if it wasn't going to last forever. Every day of winter spent inside a dry building, brought him closer to spring or summer, when it wouldn't be quite so tough back out on the streets. He knew he was more than happy with the offer, but he didn't want to make the decision for Neala.

"What do you think Neala? It's got to be better than out there at this time of the year I think." Neala took longer to reply than Lusam was expecting, and at one point he actually thought she might decline the offer. He would have to try and remember to ask her later what her hesitation was over.

"I have a question Mr Daffer," Neala said.

"Certainly, ask away," he replied smiling at her.

"I don't know about Lusam, but I'm not accustomed to being locked inside anywhere. May I ask, would we be allowed to come and go as we pleased?" Then she suddenly had another thought and added quickly, "Outside of our working hours of course."

Mr Daffer looked quite shocked at the implication that he might be suggesting enforced imprisonment, and was very quick to reply, "Of course. Of course, you may leave any time you like. All we ask is you return before ten in the evening, so we may lock up fully for the night." Then he added, "Also, we would appreciate you being as quiet as possible if you return so late. That way you won't disturb our neighbours, or indeed myself and Lucy, as we may already be asleep upstairs."

"Oh, yes. That wouldn't be a problem Mr

Daffer," Neala replied looking a little guilty. Lusam noticed Neala's question had made her a little uncomfortable, and so tried to move the conversation on swiftly.

"Thank you for your kind offer Mr and Mrs Daffer. We would both be very happy to accept your offer, and abide by your rules while we are your guests here," Lusam replied smiling at them both.

"Very good. There are a few other minor details we must discuss before you start work of course, but they can wait until later. We were just about to eat some lunch. Nothing too grand I'm afraid, only cold meat and bread, but you are both welcome to join us for something to eat, if you haven't already eaten that is" suggested Mr Daffer, looking slightly more relaxed than when they had first entered his shop. Lusam and Neala looked at each other, but neither of them needed to discuss the prospect of free food, so they agreed more than readily to Mr Daffer's offer of lunch.

"That sounds great. Thank you Mr and Mrs Daffer," replied Lusam.

"Firstly though, we would greatly appreciate you having a wash, and changing into those clean clothes Lucy has for you over there on the counter," Mr Daffer said, pointing over towards where Lucy was still standing. "You may use the wash basin in the room at the back of the shop. It's not a large room, but you should also be able to change your clothes in there."

"Okay, thanks," they both replied, and they went to gather the clothes Lucy had prepared for them on the shop counter.

Lusam suggested Neala get washed and changed first. While he waited he noticed for the first time just how big the shop actually was. Book cases lined all the walls, and there were several long rows of free standing book cases that formed long corridors lined with books. He was wondering just how long it might take to actually read them all, when his day-dreaming was interrupted by Neala informing him that it was his turn.

"Thanks," he replied, and entered the small wash-room to get himself washed and changed. Lucy walked over to Neala and asked for the clothes to be given to her for washing, then suggested Neala should make her way into the dining room and make herself comfortable, as they would be eating lunch in a few minutes.

Several minutes later Lusam joined Neala in the dining room, now dressed in a clean white shirt, brown trousers, and a pair of shiny boots. The boots were a little on the large side for his feet, but were still much better than the ones he had been wearing.

Neala looked him up and down and raised an eyebrow, smiling at him as he entered, before playfully teasing him with, "You certainly scrub up well."

"You too," was the only witty reply he could come up with, just as Mr Daffer reappeared through a set of double doors at the other end of the dining room.

"Ah, much better," Mr Daffer said, referring to the fresh appearance of his new employees. Less than a minute later Lucy entered the room through the same double doors carrying a large platter of meat, bread and cheese. She then placed it in the centre of the large table, and took her seat next to Mr Daffer. At the mere sight of the food in front of him, Lusam's stomach reminded him loudly, and not too subtly that it must indeed be time to eat.

"Please, help yourself," Lucy said, indicating towards the food on the table. After thanking them both again for their hospitality, Lusam and Neala both helped themselves to some food, and a drink of lemonade that Lucy informed them she had made herself. It was actually rather good, and Lusam commented on the fact that it was so tasty. That seemed to make Lucy very happy, and so she proceeded to explain in great detail the process of making such a sweet tasting beverage.

After the meal was over Lucy excused herself, saying she had other duties to attend to, and left them both with Mr Daffer in the dining room. During lunch, Mr Daffer had informed them that he had already taken two mattresses down to the basement, for them to use in whichever rooms they decided to take as their accommodation during their stay at the

The Old Inkwell. He suggested they all went downstairs into the basement so he could show them around, and also explain exactly what he would like to be done with the books there. Lusam and Neala followed Mr Daffer through the double doors and into a long corridor, which had several doors leading off to the left and right. At the end of the long corridor there was a large wide wooden staircase that curved around, before disappearing up onto the floor above. The walls were made of dark wood panelling, but it didn't make the corridor too dark as there seemed to be a large amount of colourful light flooding across the floor coming from somewhere above the staircase. As they approached the staircase, Mr Daffer stopped outside the last door on the left and took a key out of his pocket. While he was unlocking the door, Lusam glanced up to see where the light was coming from. He was amazed to see a huge crystal glass dome in the ceiling high above the staircase, lighting up the whole area below it. He was so engrossed at the amazing sight that he didn't notice Mr Daffer and Neala had already started to descend the stairs into the basement, and had to hurry to catch them up.

The stone stairs ended on a small landing, before turning and continuing down to an old heavy wooden door at the bottom. Mr Daffer opened the door, and Lusam was pleased to see someone had already lit several lanterns inside the room that lay beyond. As they stepped into the room, the sheer size of it became apparent to both Lusam and Neala, as they stood there opened mouthed looking around. They were now in a chamber bigger than any room Lusam had ever seen before. It was immense. It was instantly obvious that this place was much older than the building above ground, simply by the way it had been constructed. Huge stone blocks made up the walls, and running down the centre of the room were two lines of giant stone pillars that supported a vaulted ceiling high above. As Lusam looked up at the ceiling, he could just about make out what looked like pictures of something between the giant arches, but in the poor light of the lanterns he was unable to see exactly what they were.

There were several corridors leading away from

the main chamber in various directions, but none were lit, so it was impossible to tell how far back they extended.

"Well it's fair to say you won't be short of space down here," Mr Daffer said, gesturing towards the huge open space.

"No kidding," laughed Neala.

"Down that first passage are the sleeping cells of the monks who used to live here. There are well over a hundred rooms down that way. I suggest finding a couple close to this main area, as all the rooms that I have seen all look the same anyway. Your mattresses are here when you choose which room to put them in, and there are also some blankets here," he said, pointing to the pile in the corner of the room. "If you both follow me, I will show you where the books that I need you to catalogue are being stored," Mr Daffer said, as he walked towards the second corridor.

They walked past many doors on the way down the corridor. When they finally reached the end it opened out into another large room. This room was maybe a quarter of the size of the big room, but it was still huge, and almost half full of books, which were stacked almost to the ceiling. Lusam had been expecting new books, or at least recently bought books to catalogue, but these books looked very old indeed.

"And here we are," stated Mr Daffer. "These are the books I need you to catalogue. There is a desk over there with plenty of parchment, pens and ink," he said pointing to a very old writing desk in the opposite corner of the room. "I think the best way to do this would be to list them alphabetically. Now, because we have no idea how many books start with each letter of the alphabet, it would be easier to use a different piece of parchment for each letter of the alphabet. You will probably also come across some books written in a foreign language, please just make a separate list of these books and I will decide later what to do with them. Please can you also stack the books alphabetically as you record them, so we have a pile, or several piles for each letter of the alphabet. It will make finding any book much easier in the future, and as you can see, we aren't short of space."

"Sounds easy enough," replied Lusam. "If you don't mind me asking Mr Daffer, where did all these books come from?"

"When I took over the *Old Ink Well* about a year ago, I was curious about this place down here. When I was a boy, I asked my uncle many times about the monks who once lived here. He told me that they had been a very secretive cult, and nobody really knew very much about them. None of their order ever left their ranks, and the temple above ground was only the public face of their cult down here. So when I inherited this place, I started to explore a little down here. Eventually I came across several rooms where I found these books, and I moved them all into this larger room over several weeks."

"These books sure do look old," said Neala picking one up and blowing off a pile of dust, then instantly wishing she hadn't, when she started sneezing uncontrollably.

Mr Daffer laughed, and replied, "Yes, I believe

some of them are very old indeed. Most will be worthless I'm sure, but maybe among them is a valuable book or two that will make it worth my while paying your wages."

"I hope so too," replied Lusam, looking at the gigantic pile of books now facing them.

"I think now would be a good time to find the rooms you plan on using, and make them comfortable for tonight. I will bring down a good supply of lantern oil, so you'll have no chance of running out later. I have spoken to Lucy, and she agreed that you should join us for the evening meal tonight, but after today, food is something you must provide for yourselves, using your own coin. If the main shop door is locked, there will be a spare key hanging on the hook behind the door. Please make sure the door is locked, and the key is returned to the hook. Do you have any more questions before I leave you for now?" he asked.

Lusam and Neala looked at each other, and with a shake of their heads let Mr Daffer know they were happy to do as he suggested. Mr Daffer told them he would come back when the evening meal was ready, and left them to prepare their sleeping arrangements. Neala let out a quiet sigh to herself, but Lusam heard it, and noticed she looked a little concerned about something.

"What's the matter Neala? Have you changed your mind about being here?"

"No," she replied quickly. "It's not that. It's just … well, that's a lot of books, and you know I can't read. I just don't want to be useless here that's all. It's not fair taking half of the money if I can't do anything."

Lusam Laughed. "You sound just like me. Wasn't it you who told me that kind of sentiment just means you will go hungry?" he said with a smug look on his face. "Besides, I've been thinking a lot about that small problem, and I think I have the answer to it. I'll simply have to teach you to read. We will have plenty of time here in the evenings for me to teach you, and you never know, it might help you a great deal in the future."

Neala smiled at Lusam then replied, "That's very kind of you, but I'm sure learning to read will take a long time. This job would probably be long finished before I was any help to you."

"Of course it might take a while, but I know how we can make a good start, even before you can read. One thing we're not short of here is space, so it would be easy to make a pile of books for each letter of the alphabet, even before we catalogue them. I'll ask Mr Daffer for some chalk or charcoal, then I'll write each letter of the alphabet on the wall spaced out evenly around the room. It will be a simple matter of picking up a book, and matching the first letter of the title with the letter written on the wall. If we do it that way, you can help sort out the books no problem."

Neala looked at him, and ever so slightly shook her head. "Do you know Lusam, sometimes I think you are just *too* smart for your own good," she said, trying to hide the smile that appeared on her face as she turned away, but not quite managing it.

Neala had already set off towards the the main chamber when she called to Lusam. "Come on Mr Brains, let's go find our bedrooms," she said, looking back over her shoulder at him, and giving him a cheeky wink.

Mr Daffer certainly hadn't been exaggerating about the number of sleeping cells in that particular area of the underground structure. They had checked over a dozen rooms before they had to agree with Mr Daffer, that they were all pretty much the same as each other, and decided to take two rooms near the main chamber as he had suggested earlier. They did find a few locked cells, but most were open. Each cell consisted of a raised sleeping platform, where they could place the mattresses provided by Mr Daffer, a couple of hooks on the wall, and most had a small open chest to store clothes and other belongings at the side of the door. Luxurious it was not, but it was dry and surprisingly warm, considering the time of year, and the lack of any visible heat source.

Once they had placed the mattresses in their chosen cells, Lusam suggested taking a couple of extra lanterns from the main chamber, to hang on the hooks in their cells for later use.

After hanging the first lantern Neala frowned slightly, she gestured towards the unlit lantern and said, "We'll have to ask Mr Daffer for some flint, so we can light these things, I guess."

"Oh, don't worry about that," Lusam replied with a mischievous grin. He looked at the lantern Neala had just hung up, and it suddenly burst into life with a slight pop, illuminating the room in a soft yellow glow. Neala literally fell off the bed with surprise as it magically lit itself, then she quickly turned to Lusam and thumped him on the arm.

"Ouch! What was that for?" he asked rubbing his arm.

"Don't do things like that! You scared me half-to-death. I'm not used to seeing things like that happen. Try to give me some warning in future," she said, still sitting on the floor. A moment later they both fell about in fits of laughter at each others' expense.

When he finally got his breath back from laughing so hard, he managed a half-hearted, "Sorry."

"So you should be!" replied Neala, with no real

conviction behind her words.

"We probably have at least a couple of hours left until Mr Daffer will call us for the evening meal. Maybe we should start your reading lessons? We could just start with the letters of the alphabet, so it will make it easier tomorrow when we start to sort through all those books," Lusam suggested.

Although part of her was very apprehensive about trying to learn to read, in case she made a fool of herself in front of Lusam, another part of her was even more concerned that she might be useless in the task that faced them, especially if she didn't at least try and learn to read. So with much more enthusiasm than she actually felt, she replied, "Okay, that sounds good. Let's go." She stood up dusting off her trousers, and they both left the small room and headed back to the book room.

Lusam started by writing a single capital letter, and its associated lower case letter on a sheet of parchment. Then he repeated the process for each letter of the alphabet on a different piece of parchment. He thought this wouldn't be a waste of parchment, as they could reuse each sheet to list the books of that corresponding letter, when they started sorting out the books tomorrow.

Lusam was surprised at how fast Neala memorized each letter of the alphabet, and was keen to praise her fast progress. Neala also seemed happy with the swift progress she was making, and the praise being rained down on her seemed to spur her on to even faster gains.

By the time Mr Daffer came downstairs to call them for the evening meal, Neala was naming the letters of the alphabet confidently, without many mistakes at all.

"I hope you've both settled in well down here. I know it's not the most hospitable place, but if there's anything you need to make it more so, just let me know, and I'll do what I can," Mr Daffer said, leading them back up the stairs towards the main shop.

"Actually, we were quite surprised how comfortably warm it is down there. I was planning to ask you where the heat came from, as I couldn't see any reason for it to be that temperature?" asked Lusam, as they reached the first landing area.

"I'm afraid that's one question I can't answer for you. I have looked for the source of heat myself in the past, but it seems to come directly from the blocks of stone that make up the walls and floors themselves. What I found even stranger, was that in the summer months it actually gets cooler down there. Something seems to be keeping it at a constant temperature, so it never becomes too hot, or too cold. What that is, I have no idea. Feel free to have a look around and see if I missed any obvious source of heat, but I'm pretty sure there isn't one."

"That does sound strange," agreed Lusam. "While I remember, would it be possible to get either some chalk or charcoal for tomorrow please? It would speed up the cataloguing of the books quite a bit I think."

"Of course, I'll get you some after we eat, no problem at all." Turning towards Neala, Mr Daffer then said, "In the meantime, Lucy has got your clean clothes back from the laundry in town, so you may wish to change back into them before dinner."

"Thanks, I will. And thanks for the loan of these clothes too. Sorry, I may have got the trousers a little dirty on the backside though," Neala said glaring at Lusam, who found it hard to keep a straight face, as the image of her falling off the bed flashed into his mind again.

"Oh, don't worry, I'm sure they will be in the next batch that goes off to the laundry anyway," replied Mr Daffer, as they entered the main shop area.

Early the following morning, Lusam and Neala went out to the bakery to get some breakfast with the money Mr Daffer had given them the night before. They didn't spend long outside, and ate the freshly baked bread as they walked back to the shop. They wanted to make a good start that day, and catalogue as many of the books as they could. That way they could estimate how long the overall job might take them, just in case Mr Daffer happened to ask them later.

Earlier, Mr Daffer had given Lusam some chalk, and he had used it to carefully mark out the letters of the alphabet on the walls around the book room. They both picked up a few books at a time, and placed them on the floor in front of the corresponding first letter of the book's title. After several back-aching hours of bending over to pick up books, walking around the large room, and bending down to place the books on the floor again, they had maybe three hundred or so books laid out on the floor. Looking over at the gigantic pile of books that still remained, it was obvious this wasn't going to be an easy, or fast job, Lusam thought to himself.

"We should ask Mr Daffer if he has a wheelbarrow that we could use later. We could load it up with a lot more books than we can carry by hand. It should make the work much easier, and much faster," suggested Neala.

"That's a great idea," agreed Lusam, turning around and teasing her with, "Now who's the smart one?" Neala's face flushed slightly, as she smiled back at him. "I think maybe I should start writing down some of these book titles now, before the piles get too high. Maybe you should take a break for a while?" he suggested, noticing how hot and sweaty her face had become, whilst carrying so much weight non-stop for hours. He certainly needed to take a break, but bravado would have kept him going if she had refused.

"If you insist, but I'm happy to keep going for a while longer," she offered in reply.

"I don't know about you, but all that fetching and carrying has made me quite hungry. Maybe you could go out and get us something to eat? I could come with you if you prefer, but it may be better if I stay here and start to catalogue these books, just in case Mr Daffer comes down here," he said, gesturing towards the numerous piles of books, all now neatly stacked in alphabetical order.

"Yeah, that sounds like a good idea. It would be nice to get outside in the fresh air again for a while," she replied, with much more enthusiasm than he had expected. "Okay, I won't be too long," she said. And with a spring in her step, she exited the room and headed back towards the main stairs.

Lusam, with a slight groan, went over to the first pile of books and retrieved several of them, before heading back to his writing desk and recording their titles. As he began writing, he suddenly realised that they were going to need to use another part of the room, and they would also need another set of letters writing on the wall, to store the books that were already catalogued. He arranged the new area of the room while Neala was out getting their food, and continued to catalogue the books until she returned with lunch.

Neala came back with a variety of foods. She had also had managed to get some water bottles from somewhere, and even fill them with nice cool water. Very grateful for both, Lusam took his share and found an area to sit and eat his lunch, whilst thanking Neala for thinking about their water situation.

After they ate lunch they both went back to work, stacking more books, then cataloguing them over and over until it was time to stop for the day. They were both very tired, but still decided they would go out for something to eat, before returning to their sleeping cells and falling asleep, warm and content.

The next few days followed the same pattern as the first, except now Neala would buy enough food at breakfast time to last them the rest of the day, saving them a trip out in the cold evenings. The time they saved, was now spent teaching Neala how to read and write. Lusam was impressed by the speed at which Neala had picked up the basics, and by the end of the first week, she could read simple sentences with little difficulty.

They had managed to get a wheelbarrow, of sorts, from Mr Daffer a few days earlier, and it had indeed made the job of moving and re-stacking the books much faster and easier for them both. The downside, however, was that Neala now had much more free time while Lusam was writing, and she was starting to get a little bored during the extended periods of inactivity.

"Would you mind if I went to explore this place

for a bit, while you're doing that?" she asked Lusam hopefully.

"No, not at all. Just don't get lost down here," Lusam replied jokingly. He had been wondering earlier if Neala was beginning to get fed up of just standing around watching him, while he catalogued all the books; obviously she was a little. *Exploring the underground chamber would be good for her*, he thought to himself.

"Take your time. I'll be about an hour doing this pile," he said, nodding towards the stack of books closest to him. "Oh, and one other thing," he added.

"Yes?"

"Don't you dare bring back any more books," he said laughing.

Laughing right back she replied, "You can count on that!"

Neala picked up one of the spare lanterns and turned back to Lusam. "Do you mind?" she asked, nodding towards the lantern, which suddenly burst into life with a small popping sound. "Thanks," she said, heading out of the room towards the main chamber.

"No problem," he replied after her, before returning to the task at hand.

Neala had been secretly itching to explore the underground complex ever since they had first arrived. All those chambers, corridors and rooms must hold something of interest she mused to herself. Even if it was only a long forgotten coin or two. She stood in the main chamber, trying to decide how she could best explore this giant underground structure. She chose to start with the first corridor where their sleeping cells were situated. Although they had already looked inside a few of the cells down that corridor when they first arrived, they weren't really looking for anything other than a room to sleep in at the time. She also remembered several locked doors along that corridor, and after all, Mr Daffer had given them permission to explore the place. His exact words being: "*Feel free to have a look around ...*" which Neala was more than happy to interpret as: *search wherever you want.*

After thirty minutes fruitlessly searching the open cells that ran the length of the corridor, she decided to turn her attention to the locked cells instead. Neala had already decided that if the locked cells contained anything Mr Daffer had obviously stored there she would stop, and not open any more locked doors, restricting her search to only the open cells.

All her life she had grown up in the thieves' guild, and these locks were no match for her lock-picking skills. Almost at will the locks clicked open, one after another, only to reveal yet another empty room. The biggest prize she had found so far was a plate of fossilized food, and an old moth-eaten robe hanging from one of the hooks, but she wasn't about to give up just yet. Several locked cells later, she actually came across a few coins left in the bottom of a small chest. Nothing much, only a few coppers, but at least it was better than nothing. Picking them up, she continued opening the locked doors and searching the remaining cells, but she didn't find anything else of real value.

She was about to leave this corridor and try the next one along, when she realised Mr Daffer would probably remember that several of these cells once had locked doors. Even though he had, in a way, given them permission to search the structure, Neala didn't really want him knowing she'd picked the locks on these doors, and decided she best relock the ones she had opened, before moving on to the next corridor.

Neala made her way back to the main chamber again, before taking the next corridor along. She worked her way along the new corridor, just as she had the first. She noticed that the stone floors in both corridors were well-worn down the centres. They must have seen centuries of foot traffic to show so much wear and tear, she thought to herself. After another thirty minutes, Neala finally reached the end of the second corridor, but with little more to show for her efforts, than she had found in the first set of cells.

When she reached the very end of the corridor, instead of a door like there had been in the first corridor, she was faced with a solid stone wall instead. Carved into the stone wall, was a huge five pointed star, but nothing much else. She stood there looking at the strange wall and her immediate surroundings for several more minutes, before deciding that it must be time to return to the book room to help Lusam. She could always restart her exploration tomorrow, she told herself as she headed back towards the main chamber.

Back in the book room, Lusam had only just finished cataloguing the last batch of books, and had just started fetching books from the main pile again, when Neala entered the room carrying her lantern.

"How did it go? Find anything interesting on your travels?" Lusam asked, putting a pile of books down and sorting through them.

"Well, I'm not sure really. There's a wall at the end of that second corridor with a star carved into it, but there's something strange about it, and I can't quite put my finger on it," she replied, with a thoughtful look on her face.

"A wall doesn't sound very interesting to me,"

Lusam laughed. "And here I was, hoping you were going to tell me you'd found a great treasure room, full of gold and gems, and we could stop moving books around and go live like kings and queens instead."

"If only! Unless four copper coins and a stale sandwich counts as treasure I'm afraid we're still stuck with moving books, Your Highness," she said, bowing deeply to him. Standing up from behind his writing desk he laughed at her dramatic bow, then suggested they sort out more books from the main pile before they took a break to eat.

"Okay," Neala replied, still deep in thought.

Several minutes passed, and Lusam noticed how quiet Neala had been since returning to the book room. He was about to ask her what was on her mind, when she suddenly dropped the pile of books she'd been carrying onto the floor, and blurted out, "Wait here, I'll be right back!"

She then grabbed a lit lantern and ran from the room without saying another word. Lusam was more than a little curious as to why Neala had just run away like that, and was just about to pick up a lantern himself and try to follow her, when she came running back into the room again, slightly out of breath.

"Come with me! I have something important to show you," she said between breaths, and jogged back out of the room again, with Lusam following close behind her. Neala took him to the end of the second corridor where the stone wall stood, pointed and said, "Look, do you see it?"

"See what? All I see is a stone wall with a star carved into it, like you said."

"That's what I thought when I first saw it, but something didn't seem quite right to me. In the corridor where we sleep, there is a room at the end of the hallway, not a wall."

"Maybe they just didn't want to build a room at the end of this corridor," he suggested, looking at Neala as if she had gone a little crazy.

"Yes, that was my first thought too, but in the book room while I was puzzling over what I had seen here, I realised something. Look at the floor. It's been well-worn all the way to the wall. If this wasn't some kind of door that people had walked through a lot in the past, there wouldn't be any signs of wear so close to the wall itself."

Lusam looked at the floor, and had to admit, it did look like it had been worn down like the rest of the corridor behind them, but he couldn't see how the stone wall could possibly be opened.

"When I first came here, I noticed these round marks on the wall. Maybe pressing them opens the door?" Neala said, pointing to two small round indentations carved into the walls, one each side of the corridor, but too far apart for one person to press both at the same time.

"Maybe we should try it. You press the left one, I'll press the right and let's see what happens," suggested Lusam. They both pressed their thumbs to the mark, but nothing happened.

"So much for that theory," said Lusam. "Wait! Isn't that another mark on the floor back there?" he said, pointing back down the corridor several paces.

Walking back to take a look, Neala agreed, "Yes, it looks the same to me, but how will it be possible to press all three at the same time?"

"I'm not sure, let me think about this a minute. Assuming it's actually a door at all, and those indentations are in fact the way to open it ..." His statement trailed off into nothing, as he thought about the possibility of this actually being a door. Looking around he couldn't see any other obvious way to open the wall, so he decided to try a long shot, and use his mage-sight, just in case it was operated via magic. He was stunned to see not three indentations, but five. They had missed seeing the other two high up on the ceiling, which now glowed a bright green in the darkness, the same as the other three; five indentations, for the five pointed star.

Gasping in disbelief, he said, "You're right, it is a door! I can see it glowing when I use my mage-sight, and there are also another two indentations up there on the ceiling. That makes five in total, one for each point of that star."

Chapter Four

Shiva sat behind his luxuriously carved desk at the back of his small smoky office, half-hidden by the low amount of light the single small desk lamp gave off. He was looking over the reports of a recent robbery they had carried out on a local nobleman's house two nights previously in Stelgad. What he read didn't please him at all.

He had obtained reliable information that there would be several very expensive and rare jewels in the house when the robbery took place. No one but himself and his closest lieutenants had known about the jewels. He had always kept information like that secret, and only a trusted select few within his organization were ever privy to such information. He had always found it to be the best way of avoiding any information being leaked accidentally by a member of his guild. It's a well known fact, that too much drink can make a man's tongue wag too much, and in the wrong company, that could cost him a lot of money, or far worse.

He checked the report again, carefully going through the list of items obtained, but there was no mention of the jewels. That could only mean either the information he had paid a good price to obtain was incorrect, or at least one of the three men he sent to do the job had stolen the jewels for themselves.

The informant Shiva had bought the information from, he'd used several times before, and he had proved to be very reliable in the past with his information. Since he had crushed his main rivals the Crows' guild two months earlier, many of the informants who used to work for them had approached his guild with information they wished to sell. If the Crows' guild had still been around, he might have thought that they'd got to the jewels before he'd managed to obtain them. But there wasn't any competition left in Stelgad. Not since he had wiped out the Crows' guild, as well as another three smaller guilds.

He would make sure the informant hadn't indeed sold him false information, by the usual painful methods, of course, but he simply could not allow any member of his own guild to steal from him. He would have to make an example out of whoever was responsible, so nobody would ever want to steal from him again.

Two of his best men stood guard inside the doorway; one each side of the heavy oak door. Shiva wasn't concerned about any threat to his life from the outside world, here, so deep in his headquarters. The main threat to a leader in his position always came from within. Usually some young thief with a little too much ambition, and not enough skill or brains to be much of a threat. But occasionally, within a guild there would be a genuine attempt for the leadership role, and that posed much more of a threat.

Shiva had been in charge of the Hawks' guild for just over ten years now. His fast and brutal rise to power had become legendary amongst the thieves of Stelgad, and even further afield. Many had tried to remove him from his position over the last decade, both from inside his own guild, and also rival guilds, but all had failed. He ruled with a steel fist, and any who crossed him usually paid with their lives, or worse.

As he sat there, contemplating exactly which method of killing the traitorous thief would be the most painful, and the most extravagant for any witnesses, he heard a quiet knock at his door. He looked at one of his guards, who turned towards the door and slid a small spyhole open, enabling him to safely see who was on the other side.

"It's Skelly sir," the big guard informed his boss.

Shiva nodded his head once to indicate the guard could let him enter, and sat back in his chair to await his lieutenant.

Skelly was a very average looking man in every way, average height, build and looks. Every way except his cold steely blue eyes, which could scare anyone half-to-death with a single look. He was one of Shiva's best lieutenants, and exceptionally deadly with a dagger. Skelly entered Shiva's smoky office, casually nodding his head in greeting. He then stood at the opposite side of his desk waiting for the door to be closed behind him, making sure no one outside the room would overhear their conversation. When the door was finally closed he spoke to Shiva.

"Do you remember the horse that was stolen from us about two months back?" Skelly asked.

"Yeah, what about it?"

"Well, it turned up this morning. A local horse-trader that we buy from spotted it for sale over in Helveel a few days ago. He recognized the brand on it as ours, and thought we might be interested in the information. I told him that he would be compensated well, if his information checked out."

Shiva had almost forgotten about the horse, but being reminded of it now only served to enrage him even more. Just how did people expect to steal from him, and still live to tell the tale? Shiva's hand came crashing down on his desk in anger.

"I want you to choose one of our men and go with him to Helveel. Find this fool who thinks they can steal from me and get away with it. Question the horse-trader where our horse was seen, and find out what he knows. Find out who is responsible, and bring them here to me—alive!" he almost shouted, banging his fist down on his desk again.

"No problem," Skelly replied calmly.

"Remember, I want them alive when you deliver them to me. Do you understand?"

"Yeah, don't worry, I won't cut off anything too important," he replied with a slight grin. Skelly was the only person in the whole guild who could possibly get away with a comment like that, and he knew it. Although, he wondered if even he had gone too far with the dark mood Shiva was in at the moment. Nothing else was said between them, so Skelly just nodded and turned towards the door, before departing Shiva's office. Skelly quickly recruited another well known assassin within the guild, and they made plans to leave for Helveel, to bring back the *fool* who had stolen Shiva's property.

He certainly wouldn't want to be in their shoes when Shiva got a hold of them.

Chapter Five

Lusam and Neala quietly stood looking at the huge star carved into the stone wall, wondering just what great treasures might have been hidden behind it centuries before.

"Well, are we going to try and open it or what?" asked Neala impatiently.

"What happens if it's booby-trapped?" Lusam asked. "They obviously went to a lot of trouble to hide this place when it was in use, whenever that was. Surely it has some kind of defensive measures in place, in case anyone tries to steal whatever is in there."

"Maybe," agreed Neala, "but there again, with those two indentations right up there on the ceiling, who would know how to get inside in the first place?"

"Hmm. Just how *are* we going to press those two up there anyway? Or for that matter, how are we going to press all five at the same time?" Lusam asked, gesturing to the very well spaced out indentations.

"I'm not sure. I was hoping you had a plan for that," Neala replied.

"Well I suppose I could try pressing them magically. I was taught by my grandmother how to move things with magic, and although I've never tried manipulating five things at the same time, I could give it a go."

"Sure, that sounds like a good idea. But, can you do that from a distance? If you can, maybe we should move further back down the corridor, in case you're right, and it is booby-trapped."

"Good idea," agreed Lusam, as they retreated to what they judged would be a safe distance, before he tried to activate the opening mechanism. Lusam concentrated on the five points and applied pressure magically to them all at the same time, but nothing happened. He tried to press harder, but still nothing moved.

"It's not working. I'm pressing them all but nothing is happening. Maybe it's a combination lock, or maybe I have to press them in a certain order?" he said out loud, but mainly to himself. He worked out the number of possible combinations in his head, then with a groan said, "If it is actually a combination of the five indentations, there would be one hundred and twenty permutations. That's going to take some time and planning, to make sure we don't miss any combination."

"How long will it take to open if it is a combination lock?" Neala asked impatiently, looking at the wall, and dreaming of what could be behind it.

"That depends. If we're incredibly lucky, we could get the correct combination on the first attempt, or if we are equally unlucky, it could be the last attempt. Then there's the possibility that if the combination is entered incorrectly once, or several times, it may lock out further attempts for a set period of time, or even permanently. It could even trigger that supposed booby-trap. The truth is, it's simply impossible to know exactly how long it would take to open, and that's even if it is a combination lock in the first place," replied Lusam, sounding slightly defeated even before they had begun.

"Can't you just blast through it with your magic powers?"

Laughing at the imagined destruction, he replied, "I wouldn't know how to, and besides, even if I did know how, we couldn't destroy Mr Daffer's property like that anyway."

"I know, I wasn't serious about blasting through. It's just so annoying being this close, and not being able to see what's behind this damn door!"

"Yeah, I know what you mean," he agreed. "I suppose we better start working out all the combinations if we're going to try this. That way, we don't miss any." He turned and started heading back towards the main chamber again.

"Could the star have any clues to the combination?" Neala suggested, as they began walking back.

Lusam thought about it a few moments. "Of course, the star! You're a genius Neala," he said, jumping with excitement.

"What about the star?" Neala asked confused.

"A five pointed star, and five indentations. Look at how the star is created on the wall. It's been drawn in one continuous line, without beginning or end. All the points of the star are connected. Maybe all I need to do is magically connect the indentations with each other, just like the star, and not just press them," Lusam said excitedly.

"It's worth a try," Neala agreed.

Lusam cleared his mind, and concentrated on connecting the indentations magically in the same configuration the star had been created. He wasn't sure exactly how he could do it. He finally concentrated on the image of what he wanted, and let the power flow out of him. A green line of power burst into life, connecting each of the indentations with the next, and creating a perfect five pointed star to mirror the one on the wall. With a grinding sound, and a flurry of dust, the wall, very slowly, started to move on its own.

"You did it!" shouted Neala excitedly, hugging and kissing him on the cheek at the same time.

"Yeah, looks like it. You'll have to find me more doors to open if you're going to do that every time," he said, grinning at her. She just smiled back at him, and they waited for the door to fully open, trying to be as patient as was humanly possible.

When the door had finally fully opened, and the dust settled, Neala said, "Maybe I should go in alone first."

"Why?" he asked, confused at her request.

"Well, seeing as you're the only one who can open this door with magic, it makes sense for me to go inside first, just in case the door closes again and traps me inside. Then you could let me back out again. If we both go in together, who would let us both out?" she said, as if it was the most obvious thing in the world.

Lusam laughed. "That's a good point," he agreed. "The only problem is, there may be other dangers in there that you can't see, but I might be able to with my mage-sight. I suggest you take a lantern and enter the room. If the door remains open, wait until I enter and check the room for hidden traps before you move any further inside, just to be on the safe side."

"Hmm … I hadn't thought about that either, maybe you're right. Okay, I'll go see if the door stays open, but be ready to get me out of there if it closes fast," Neala replied, looking a little less confident than she had a moment ago.

"Sure, no problem, but if it closes even twice as fast as it opened, we would still have enough time for a picnic before we would be in any danger of getting locked inside," he chuckled.

"True," she agreed smiling back at him. She took her lantern and approached the darkened room. As she reached the entrance she held up the lantern and took a step forward into the room. As soon as her foot made contact with the floor, the whole room suddenly burst into light.

"Aargh! My eyes," she said, now shielding her eyes from the daylight-strength light emanating from the walls all around her. Lusam came running towards the room and stopped just outside the doorway, then looked tentatively inside. The room was circular in shape, with the single pedestal in the centre. On the pedestal was a single item. As Neala's eyes became accustomed to the bright light, she also took in the almost empty room. Empty apart from a single item sitting on top of the pedestal.

"OH GREAT! Just what we need, another book!" Neala said exasperated.

Lusam burst out laughing at Neala's reaction. She was obviously expecting a room full of gold,silver and gemstones, and not a single book to be so well guarded behind the almost impenetrable wall.

Lusam noticed another five indentations in the same configuration on the inside of the room, and felt confident he would be able to reopen the door from the inside, should it close automatically while they were still inside. He walked over to where the large book was placed on top of the pedestal and looked at the title. He didn't recognize the language the text was written in. He had never seen anything like it before.

"I can't read the language this is written in. I wonder what kind of book it is?" he said, looking at the ornately designed leather and metal bound cover of the book. "Maybe it's some kind of holy book that the monks used in the past," he guessed.

"Could be I guess, but if nobody can read it anymore, I guess we'll never know," replied Neala.

Lusam was curious as to what the book contained, so he took a step up onto the base of the pedestal, where he could better see the contents of the book. Reaching out he opened the book, ready to try and make sense of its contents, when a searing light stunned his whole body. He instantly turned rigid as a force-field of some kind completely surrounded his entire body. Neala noticed the sudden change and called out to him, but he was unable to respond, as he could no longer hear her calls.

"LUSAM!" she cried out. Neala reached out to grab him, and was violently thrown across the room by the force-field now surrounding him. Luckily she wasn't hurt badly and quickly got back to her feet, whilst rubbing the lump that was now forming on the back of her head. She didn't know what to do. She couldn't reach him because of the force-field, and he wasn't responding to her ever desperate calls. She also dare not leave him, in case the door closed again and trapped him inside all alone.

Panic pulsed through her with every breath she took. She hadn't known Lusam that long, but he was the best friend she had ever had. More than a friend she realised at that moment. Maybe she actually loved him, she wasn't sure. What she was sure about, was the fact she couldn't lose him. Not here. Not now. It was her stupid idea to try and open this room, and now it had resulted in this happening to Lusam.

Neala paced around and around the outside of the room, trying to think of a solution, but she could think of nothing. At one point, in sheer desperation she had sat down and cried for several minutes, before finally pulling herself together again, and once more attempting to come up with an answer, but to no avail. The passage of time was difficult to judge, but she guessed at least forty minutes had elapsed since Lusam had become trapped. She had come to the conclusion that she must risk leaving him, and get help somehow, from somewhere. She was about to leave the room when she heard, rather than saw the force-field vanish, and Lusam collapsed onto the floor clutching the now closed book to his chest.

"LUSAM!" she called to him, running over to where he'd fallen. As Lusam became more aware of his surroundings, he realised he was being hugged tightly by Neala. She was crying whilst calling his name, and apologizing over and over again.

Confused, but enjoying the attention from her, he hugged her back, and while stroking her hair asked, "What's the matter? Why are you crying? Are you okay?"

"Yes, I'm fine now. Are you hurt?" she asked, still crying on his shoulder.

"No, I'm fine, I think. I … I just know things. Things about magic that I didn't know before. Strange things. Strange, but incredible things. It's hard to explain, it's all spinning in my head at the moment."

"I was so worried about you. I was going crazy

in here looking at you just standing there, and I couldn't do anything to help you," she sobbed into his shirt.

"I don't understand. I just opened the book, and then fell onto the floor. How can you have got so worried about me?" he asked confused.

"You opened that book and some kind of force-field froze you up there on that pedestal. I tried to get you out, but I couldn't. You were stuck in there for a long time, maybe forty minutes or more, then you just collapsed onto the floor just now."

"I only remember opening the book, then I felt dizzy and fell over. It all happened in a blink of an eye for me," he replied hugging her close, as she still clung to him tightly.

"Please can we get out of here? I've had enough of treasure hunting for one day," she said.

"Sure. Come on. Let me help you up," he replied, helping her to her feet. Neala was keen to get out of the room, and hastily headed for the exit, where she waited for Lusam to join her.

Lusam walked towards the door absent-mindedly, still carrying the book clutched tightly to his chest. As he reached the threshold of the door, another force-field suddenly came in to being, and catapulted him back inside the room. The book vanished from his hands and reappeared on the pedestal again, as he landed with a thud on the floor at the base of the pedestal.

"Ouch!" he said stunned, then slowly started to stand up again.

"Are you okay?" Neala asked desperately from the doorway, obviously afraid to test if the force-field was still active.

"Yeah, I'm fine thanks," he replied, dusting off his clothes for the second time in as many minutes. Lusam walked back over to the door, and gingerly reached out towards where the force-field had just thrown him across the room. Hoping he wasn't now trapped in the room, he was very relieved to find that the force-field was now gone.

"Hmm … I guess whoever placed that book here didn't want it to leave this room. It seems I can walk out without the book just fine, but not with it."

As he turned to take one last look at the strange book, the illuminated walls fell into darkness, and the stone door began its long slow closing process.

On their way back to the book room Lusam was trying to make sense of what was now in his head. He was sure he knew the entire contents of the book somehow, and yet he didn't fully understand it. As time passed, it became easier for him to pick out individual pieces of information that he had absorbed magically from the strange book. From simple spells, to extremely complex spells, he seemed to know them all in exquisite detail.

As they entered the book room, Neala asked, "What did you mean back there when you said you knew things?"

"I was just thinking about that myself. To be honest, it's very hard even for me to understand." He stood still thinking for a few moments before continuing. "I was thinking maybe the book was some kind of special training tool. One that the monks used to teach themselves how to use magic. I'm not really sure why, but I get the feeling it's much more than that for some strange reason," he said, taking a seat at the writing desk.

"I don't suppose it taught you a fast way to clear this book mountain?" Neala said laughing, nodding towards the huge stack of books that were still piled high in the corner of the room.

Searching his new found knowledge he replied, "Actually, maybe I could speed up things a little. I discovered how to levitate things. So I could levitate the piles of books from over in the corner, and save us having to carry them by hand. That would save us some time and effort."

Lusam stood up from behind his writing desk and, without waiting for a reply from Neala, he recalled the spell for levitating objects. As began formulating the spell in his mind, a pile of around twenty large books levitated off the floor and started to float towards them. Neala jumped backwards, out of the path the books seemed to be taking, just as they started to wobble.

CRASH!

The books came tumbling down in a huge jumbled mess all over the floor.

"Oops ... Sorry," Lusam said, looking a little embarrassed.

Neala rolled her eyes at the mess, and replied, "Seems like you need to practise that a bit more."

"Yeah, I guess so," he agreed. He tried to think of an analogy to fit the way it felt to try and use the magic the book had forced into his brain. He thought for a couple of minutes, and then decided the best way he could describe how it felt was to say, "It's like believing you already know how to ride a horse, but only because you've been told how to do it, or you've seen it done by others many times before, but without actual practice riding the horse itself, you're likely to fall off a lot. If that makes any sense to you?"

"Yeah, I suppose it does," Neala agreed, then after thinking a moment she added, "Why don't you practise in the large chamber in the evenings, after my reading lessons?"

"That sounds great, as long as you're not going to be too bored. If you are, I suppose you could always explore the rest of this place while I practise my magic," Lusam said.

"No chance!" she replied very hastily. Then after a few seconds, when her natural instinct to find hidden treasure had obviously caught up with her again, she added, "Well, maybe I could just take a little look around, just to see if I can find anything interesting."

Lusam laughed at her, and he started to pick up the books he had dropped on the floor. "Just stay well away from any secret doors with big stars on them, and I'm sure you'll be just fine."

"That's not funny! I was really worried about you," Neala said. Then, keeping him guessing, she added, "I'm glad you're not stuck in that room forever anyway … it would have been hard for me to get paid from Mr Daffer, with you being the only person who can read here." She quickly turned away from him so he couldn't see the amused look on her face, and started picking up books with her back to him.

"Hey!" he said, in a pretend hurt voice. He crept up behind her and tickled her sides with both hands.

Neala squealed and dropped the books on the floor again with a echoing crash, spinning around quickly, and coming face to face with Lusam. He didn't release his grip, and they found themselves standing very close to each other, gazing into each others eyes for what seemed like hours. Then he leant forward and gently kissed her perfect lips, before whispering, "Thank you for being worried about me."

"You're welcome," she whispered back breathlessly. Then she pulled him even closer, and gave him a much more passionate kiss than he had ever thought possible.

That night he took one of the large books to his room. He knew there wasn't much chance of him sleeping after kissing Neala like that. All he could think about were her soft lips, and the way she felt pressed against him while they kissed. He really was falling in love with her, and hoped beyond hope, that she felt the same way about him. He hadn't had very much, if any, experience when it came to girls.

Growing up on the streets gave you a different set of priorities. Like where your next meal was coming from, or how to survive the latest winter storm. He didn't know if Neala had any more experience than he did, but he guessed her life must have been far less restrictive in recent years than his had been.

It was Seventh-day tomorrow, a rest day, when they both usually went for a walk in the forest. Neala had enjoyed their first trip to the forest so much, she had asked to go back several times since. Lusam would have been happy to go anywhere with Neala. Just being in her company made him feel happy. But the forest had always had a special place in his heart, and so he looked forward to their weekly trip with even more enthusiasm. The book he had brought with him to his sleeping cell was very thick and heavy, but he hadn't intended to read it.

Lusam thought that several of the spells he had acquired might be especially useful in their current situation. Part of it however, required him to be proficient with the levitation spell, the one he had failed at so miserably earlier that day, so he spent the first part of the night practising levitating the book off his bed. After a couple of hours he became very good at the spell, and decided to visit the book room to collect more books. He was curious to find out if it took more effort as the weight and number of objects were increased.

He stood up from his bed and reached for the lantern, before realising he no longer needed a lantern. With a single thought, an extremely bright sphere of light flared into existence right in front of his face, almost blinding him. He quickly cancelled the spell and returned his room back to its normal light level again. All he could see were white spots dancing in front of his eyes wherever he looked. Re-examining his knowledge of the spell, he realised that he should have created the orb above himself, and far less bright. It seemed even the simplest of spells needed a certain amount of practice to perfect them.

After ten minutes his vision seemed to have returned to normal, and he decided to try again. This time the light orb appeared above him, but the light level was still too high, so concentrating, he dimmed it to an appropriate level. Smiling to himself, he started to leave his room, only to realise the light orb had remained where he had created it. Searching his new found wealth of knowledge, he quickly applied the spell that would make the light orb follow him, and he set off again towards the book room.

When he arrived at the book room, he started his experiment by lifting a small pile of three books that were already stacked neatly on the floor. They started to float up into the air, just like the single book had done so many times in his room. Whilst moving them around the room, he found it took only fractionally more energy to move the three books, than it had the single book.

He spent the next hour or so lifting an ever increasing number of books, until he was unable to lift any more. He had found his current limit—but he was still very impressed at the number he could lift at any one time. He also noticed that moving the location of a large number of books, required more energy than just levitating them. The distance from where he was trying to levitate the books also increased the energy required, as did the number of items: if there were ten books in a pile, it was much easier to move the whole pile, than it would have been to move ten single books laid out on the floor individually.

The use of his new magical abilities had certainly had an effect on his body too. He now felt so tired he could almost have imagined he had actually moved all those books by hand, and would have been happy to have just slept where he stood. Yawning loudly, he turned and headed back to his cell. He decided that he would at least try and get some sleep, even if it was only for the few remaining hours of night that were left to him. Almost as soon as his body touched the mattress he was asleep, and dreaming of a certain girl now close to his heart.

The next morning Neala was up at her usual time, but noticed Lusam was still sleeping soundly as she past his sleeping cell. She decided not to disturb him, and instead go out to the market and get the provisions that they would need for their weekly trip to the forest. She always enjoyed visiting the market in the early mornings. It had been part of her daily duties back in Stelgad, when she'd lived in the thieves' guild known as the Crows. She had always been the one who would visit the various local traders, and arrange for the food to be delivered to a warehouse that was secretly owned by the Crows' guild. Locally the warehouse was believed to be a simple storage facility. One that would supply the local riverboat captains and road caravans with fresh produce, but in reality, it was used to supply the Crows' guild. Acquiring food using this method greatly reduced the risk of a rival guild poisoning the food supply, as it wasn't delivered directly to their guild headquarters. Some of the food was in fact sold to various riverboat captains and merchants to keep up the illusion of a supply warehouse, but most of it was destined for the dining hall of the Crows' guild.

Neala knew the freshest and best produce was always available first thing in the mornings at any market. Freshly baked breads, firm ripe fruits and vegetables were all easy to obtain, if you got to the market early enough. Being Seventh-day meant she would have to visit the market in the west quarter of town. The wealthy people chose not to work on the Seventh-day, instead having a day of rest, but it was never an option for the poorer people of the city, who always had to work hard to make enough to live.

As Neala left the book shop and turned to walk down the cobbled street towards the market in the west district, she couldn't help feeling sad at the loss of her friends and colleagues at the Crows' guild. She had spent her entire life growing up among them. And although she had never received the kind of love a normal family might give their child, she was not ill-treated in any way either. She often wondered if any of them had survived that awful night. Maybe a few lucky ones had been out on guild business, or running errands like she had been. Before meeting Lusam she had thought about going back to Stelgad almost daily, to see if anyone had survived, but knew it would be a death sentence for her if she tried. Somehow, it didn't seem to hurt as much now she'd met Lusam. Realising this was the first time she had thought about her old guild in a long time, she allowed herself a brief smile, and continued towards the marketplace.

One thing she did miss from her old life in the guild however, were the tools of her trade. She had been forced to leave everything that she owned at her old headquarters and flee the city that fateful night. The thing she missed most of all was her thick leather belt, which held her finely balanced throwing knives. When Neala first arrived in Helveel, she had fully intended to replace the throwing knives and belt, using the money she'd got from selling the stolen horse. That plan, however, didn't work out for her, as she was refused entry to one of the local guilds, and had to spend what little money she had simply to survive. Although her current job of sorting books was far less dangerous than the life of a thief, she still felt half-naked and vulnerable without the reassuring weight of her trusty throwing knives at her waist.

Having found everything she needed at the early market, Neala headed back to the the book shop with a spring in her step. She enjoyed going to the forest so much with Lusam. She always felt relaxed there, as if she belonged somehow. It was hard to explain, but in a town or city, she had always been aware of everyone and everything around her, what they were doing, how they were acting and what they were looking at. It was a good trait for any member of a thieves' guild to have: being fully aware of your surroundings, usually helped keep you alive. She never realised just how tense she must have always been in towns and cities, until she first visited the forest with Lusam, and was able to truly relax for the first time in her life.

Entering the shop she saw Lucy behind the counter writing some information down on a piece of parchment.

"Good morning Lucy," Neala said with a smile.

"Good morning to you too," Lucy replied in a quiet voice.

"Is everything okay Lucy? You don't sound yourself today."

"I'm not feeling too well at the moment, I'm afraid. Probably just a chill," Lucy replied, with a slightly forced smile.

"I hope you feel better soon. If you need anything, just let me know. I don't mind going to the apothecary if you need any medicine to make you feel better," Neala offered.

"That's very kind of you Neala, but I'm sure I'll be fine, thank you."

"Okay, if you change your mind later, you know where I am," Neala said, before heading to the stairs of the underground chamber.

Neala made her way straight to the book room, expecting to find Lusam working there while she had been gone, but she found the room was empty. When she reached his cell, she found him still in bed, asleep. Worried *he* might be ill too, she tried to wake him up gently, but he didn't seem to stir. All manner of things flashed through her head, not least of which involved the previous day's strange encounter with the book in the hidden room. Maybe it had damaged him in some way. Almost panicking, she grabbed his shoulder and tried to shake him awake. With a groan, he turned towards her, and with tired-looking eyes squinting against the light, he asked, "What's up? Wha … What time is it?"

Relieved to see him awake and well, she relaxed a little before replying, "It's mid-morning sleepy head. Time to get up. Don't forget we're going to the forest today."

The first thing Lusam noticed sitting up in bed was the enormous headache he'd woken up with, and his stomach felt emptier than he could ever remember. Seeing the parcels of food in Neala's hand was more than his stomach could take, and it let out a huge rumble.

"Good thing I went out and bought us some breakfast by the sounds of that," she said, nodding towards his over-active stomach.

"Oh, breakfast sounds wonderful!" he said, still eyeing the parcels like a hungry wolf.

After they had eaten breakfast he felt much better. Even his headache had almost subsided completely by the time they were ready to leave for their day out in the forest. Outside, there were the first signs of spring in the air. The sun was shining, and the first batch of insects had hatched and were flying around clumsily in the cool morning air, as they always did that time of year. He was under no illusions however, he knew even though it was a warm springlike day today, it could be snowing this time tomorrow if the wind changed direction again. The weather this close to the mountains was always unpredictable, but especially so during early spring and late autumn.

Lusam was hoping that last night with Neala, in the book room, was something that would be repeated again, and sooner rather than later if he had any choice in the matter. He tried to think of something intelligent to say to her. Something that wouldn't sound too forward, but everything he came up with in his mind, he thought, made him sound like a complete fool. He eventually decided to just take the plunge and hold her hand, which to his great relief, she didn't seem to mind at all.

They left Helveel via the east gate as usual, and headed towards the bridge that crossed the river, still holding hands. Once they had crossed the bridge

Lusam asked, "Would you mind if we walked along the river for a while before we go into the forest today?"

"Sure, no problem. Something on your mind?" Neala asked.

"No. Not really. I was thinking last night that maybe I could combine several of my new spells to help us out a little."

"Help us out … in what way?" she asked curiously.

"Well, Mr Daffer's job is fine, but it won't last forever. So last night I was thinking about how my new spells could earn us a living in the future. The obvious would be at carnivals performing magic tricks, but I was always told never to reveal my power to anyone, because it could be very dangerous for me."

"But, you showed me your magic in the forest with the animals," Neala said.

"Yes, but you're different. I trust you," he said smiling at her. He gestured for them to sit down on the bank of the river, and she sat down beside him.

"So what's your idea? I hope it doesn't involve levitating anything," she said giggling to herself.

He quickly looked around to make sure nobody could see them, and without a second thought, he lifted her clean off the ground and into the air, while she kicked and screamed for him to put her down immediately. Laughing at her flailing her arms and legs around in mid-air, Lusam said, "Actually, I was practising last night. I've become quite good at it. In fact, I bet I could keep you there all day. Hmm … I wonder if it's any more difficult to hold something above the water?"

"Don't you dare!" she screamed at him. "Put me down right now!"

"Only if you promise not to make fun of me anymore," he replied, still laughing at her.

"Yes! Yes! I promise. Now put me down!" she squealed.

He gently lowered her to the ground, and released his spell. WHACK! She hit his arm.

"Don't ever do that again!" she yelled at him. Neala actually looked visibly shaken by the experience, and Lusam was very hard pressed to stop laughing at her expense.

Regaining control of his amusement, he offered a half-hearted, "Sorry."

Neala glowered at him as he tried to put his most apologetic face on, but inside he still found her reaction amusing to say the least, and he was sure she could tell.

After a few minutes of silence, Neala asked, "So … are you going to tell me what you thought of last night that would help us, or not?"

"Well, as you may, or may not know, the city of Helveel is an old mining town. This river runs directly from the Elveen mountains, and it used to contain lots of gold in its sediment. It's been a long time since it's been worth panning for gold here, but I think I can collect enough gold with magic to make it worth the effort," he replied, then waited for her to start teasing him about his idea.

He was pleasantly surprised when she just calmly replied, "Do you really think you could do that?"

"Yes, I think so. I can locate any gold that's in the river magically, then levitate it off the riverbed. Once I have collected it all together, I can remove it from the river easy enough. The problem would be how to create coins or strips with it. I have a few ideas about that, but it might take a bit of practice before I get it right."

Neala was silent for what seemed like a long time, and at first Lusam thought she might be too sceptical about his idea, but he was soon proved wrong.

"Once you've got the gold out of the river, it wouldn't matter how long it took you to turn it into coins," she said nodding towards the river. "Even if you couldn't make anything out of it, the gold would still be worth money."

"Yes, I thought about that too. The problem is, if we turn up in town with a bag full of gold dust, it's likely to start a fresh gold rush around here, and then we would have to find another river to work. Not to mention all the unwanted attention we would get. I don't know about you, but I would rather do without that," he said, looking out over the sparkling water.

"Yes, I can see that might be a problem," Neala agreed. "So are you going to try it now?"

"That was the idea. I was searching the riverbed as we walked along, and I could sense gold all along its length, but here it was a bit stronger. I'm not sure what this will look like when I start the process, so I need you to keep a good lookout for anyone who might see us, and warn me if anyone approaches."

"That sounds easy enough to me. Just let me know when you're ready to start."

"No time like the present, I guess," he said, before starting the spell to locate all the gold within his range. As he concentrated he could sense thousands upon thousands of small particles of gold. There was no way he could single out each and every particle all at the same time, and then raise them from the riverbed as one. He thought about the problem for a while, then turned to Neala and said, "I think I'll have to do this a different way from the way I planned. There's a fair bit of gold here, but it's all extremely small pieces, much smaller than grains of sand. We'll need something to store it in, or the wind might just blow it away after I release it from my spell."

Looking around, it became obvious there was nothing available to store the gold dust in. Just as Lusam was about to give up and arrange to try again next week, Neala said, "What about my boot? Can you get it inside without the wind carrying it away?"

"Yes, I think I can. Let's give it a try," he said, turning back to the river. Locating the gold again he decided to work from left to right. He levitated a few hundred particles at a time from the riverbed to the surface, and then out of the river. The fine gold particles glistened in the sunlight as they arced through the air, forming a constant stream as they entered Neala's boot which lay on the riverbank. Minutes passed before Neala could see more than a glimpse of gold in the bottom of her boot.

As each particle entered the boot, Lusam released it to gravity, and then searched out the next one on the riverbed to take its place. The constant glistening stream of gold dust now leaving the river, and accumulating in Neala's right boot, looked like a faint golden rainbow stretching out into the water. Lusam kept lifting the gold out of the sediment until he could no longer maintain the spell because of the range. When he had done all he could, he lay back on the riverbank with a sigh of relief.

"How did we do?" he asked without sitting up.

"Take a look for yourself," Neala replied, holding out the boot for him to inspect the contents.

"Wow! Not bad at all," he said looking at the contents of the boot. "Maybe enough to make a couple of gold coins in there."

"I would say so too," Neala agreed.

"Give me a few minutes to rest, and then I'll try turn it into something more usable," he said, thinking about the best way to accomplish the task.

After a few minutes rest, he decided to have a go at making a coin or two from the gold dust. First, he magically separated half of the gold dust, and contained it in a small force-field so it didn't blow away with the wind. Levitating it out of the boot and away from where they were sitting, he concentrated on increasing the heat within the small force-field. Hotter and hotter the space inside the force-field became, until he could see the gold dust melt into a liquid inside the mini spherical force-field he had created. He concentrated again, and began to manipulate the shape of his force-field, recreating the shape of a coin.

This was much harder than he thought it would be, because truth be told, he hadn't seen too many gold coins in his lifetime to be very familiar with them in the first place. Eventually, he settled for the design of a silver coin which he was sure would be close enough; after all, gold was gold. Once the molten gold was pressed into the shape of a coin, he sent it out over the water and lowered it into the cold flowing river. Releasing the force-field, with a hissing sound, the coin instantly solidified into the shape of a coin. Then he lifted the, now cool, coin back out of the river, and dropped it into his hand. Looking closely at the coin, he decided he was happy with his first attempt, but knew he could improve the design with further practice. Repeating the process he created a second coin, so now he was holding two new shiny gold coins. "Not bad," he said out loud to himself.

"Are you kidding me! That was amazing! I've never seen anything like that in my life. You just created gold coins out of thin air!" Neala said, jumping around excitedly.

"Not quite out of thin air. The gold was already there in the river," he replied, grinning at her. Flipping one of the coins in her direction, she deftly caught it in mid-air with her left hand, whilst trying to put her boot back on with her right.

"You're giving me one of your gold coins?" she asked, looking a little shocked at his generosity.

"Of course, we're a team, remember?" he replied, winking at her.

She walked over to him and gave him a big hug, before saying, "Thank you Lusam."

The rest of that day they spent in the forest, where Lusam taught Neala all about the edible plants of spring, which were just starting to show themselves in places here and there, before they headed back to town a little richer, but still holding hands.

Chapter Six

The following morning Neala made her way to the book room where she expected to find Lusam already at work. He was usually the first up and liked to get a good start, even before Neala went out on her daily shopping trip to buy their breakfast and other provisions.

"Morning," said Neala, smiling at Lusam sitting at his desk, already hard at work.

"Good morning. Did you sleep well?" he asked without looking up, still concentrating on his writing. When he finished his current entry, he placed his pen safely at the side of the ink well and stood up from behind his desk, stretching out his stiff back with a groan.

"Yes thanks. How about you?" Neala replied.

"Not too bad I guess, but that mattress seems harder than the floor some nights," he replied, rubbing the base of his back.

Laughing, Neala replied, "Yeah, I know what you mean. But at least it's warmer, and drier down here."

"That's true," he agreed, smiling at her.

"I was wondering if you wouldn't mind if I took a little longer today when I went out for our supplies?" she asked hopefully.

"Of course not. Did you have something else planned for today?" Lusam asked curiously.

"Well … when I was forced to leave Stelgad in such a hurry, I had to leave some important things behind. I wasn't able to retrieve my belt of throwing knives, and I really miss having them. I've been thinking, because you gave me that gold coin yesterday, I might be able to call in at the blacksmith's shop and get some replacements made."

"Sure, it's your money to do with as you wish," he replied, forcing a smile onto his face. No matter how hard he tried, he could never imagine Neala as a cold killer, wielding daggers and throwing knives, but he knew first hand how deadly she was with such weapons, even if it had only been in self-defence.

"Thanks Lusam. I won't be too long I hope, maybe an extra hour at the most. See you soon," she said, turning and heading out of the book room with a spring in her step. Lusam waved as she left, and then went back to his desk to continue his work, cataloguing the seemingly never-ending book mountain.

Neala opened the door at the top of the stairs and stepped into the shop. Seeing Lucy at the counter, she noticed that she looked even worse than when she'd seen her the day before.

"Good Morning Lucy. You really don't look well today. Maybe you should go and sit down. I can help you with whatever you're doing," Neala said, concerned at her pale looking face, and the sweat beads on her forehead.

"Oh … good morning Neala. I'm fine thank

you. I just haven't felt myself these last few days, but I'm sure it will pass soon. I prefer to keep busy rather than mope around, but thanks for offering your help, I appreciate it," Lucy replied, trying hard to look more energetic than she actually felt.

"Okay, if you're sure. But don't over do it working too hard. You need to rest, not work," Neala chastised, sounding more like Lucy's mother than her employee.

Lucy smiled and nodded her agreement, then continued with what she was doing before Neala had arrived. Neala looked back at Lucy as she left the shop, and wondered if she would take her advice to rest, before coming to the conclusion that Lucy was a grown woman, and could make her own decisions. Closing the shop door gently behind her, Neala started down the now familiar cobbled road towards the local Blacksmith shop, all the time tightly clutching the shiny new gold coin in her pocket, like a child on their way to a sweet shop.

Neala had discovered there were three blacksmith shops in Helveel. One was in the north quarter, where all the rich traders and high-born lived. She doubted the blacksmith in that part of town had ever been asked to make a set of throwing knives in his life, not that she could have afforded to buy them there even if he had. The second was in the south district, and although the price there should be more to her liking, she had been advised against using that blacksmith, as he specialized mainly as a horse farrier, and was known locally for the poor quality of his metals. The only real option was the third blacksmith, who was located in the west quarter of the city. Thinking back to the last time she and Lusam had ventured through the streets of the west quarter, she cringed to herself at the thought of visiting that part of the city again. She remembered what Lusam had told her, that during the day the streets were as safe as the rest of the city, but that didn't stop her feeling nervous about venturing back into that part of Helveel alone.

The streets in the west quarter seemed eerily quiet at this time of the morning. Neala imagined most of the trade in this part of the city was conducted during the hours of darkness for various reasons. She turned a corner and noticed a seedy looking tavern with a sign hanging outside. There were two old drunks standing outside the open tavern door, leaning on each other for stability, and singing old sea faring songs, badly. Looking at the sign, she realised for the first time in her life that she could actually read what the words said: '*The Ferret Hole*.'

Feeling very pleased with herself, Neala continued along the cobbled street until reaching a junction, where she took a sharp right turn. After walking for several more minutes, she began to get the district feeling that she was being followed. Looking back the way she had come, she searched the doorways and shadows for anyone that may be trying to hide there, but couldn't see any sign of anyone. Either her over-active imagination was playing tricks on her, or whoever was following her was very good at their job.

Using the reflections in the glass shop windows as she passed, she tried to catch a glimpse of anyone who might be following her, but still she couldn't see any sign of anyone sneaking around behind her. Not knowing if the threat was real, or simply in her head, she decided not to take any chances, and increased her pace a little. As she turned the next corner, she set off at a jog down the wide street, still checking all the reflections and listening for anyone following as she went. When Neala finally reached what was classed as the main area of commerce in the west district, she started to relax, as she joined the small crowds of people going about their daily business of buying and selling their wares. Checking one last time, she still couldn't see anyone following her, but decided she would take the much longer route back, through the north quarter of the city, when she later returned to the book shop.

The blacksmith's shop was easy enough to find. A sign depicting a hammer and anvil hung above the door, swinging gently in the light morning breeze. The large well-oiled door opened with ease and operated a bell as it did so, alerting the owner to her presence in the shop. Less than a minute later a very muscular middle-aged man with dark hair, and a beard peppered with grey appeared from the back of the shop. Looking at him, Neala judged him to be in his mid-to-late forties. Still wearing his apron and holding a strange looking hammer he nodded to Neala, looking her up and down, before saying, "Hello there! Is there something I can help you with?"

"Yes, I hope so. I was told you made weapons here?"

The man looked at her again, this time with a little more curiosity in his eyes. It was obvious he was used to being asked for weapons, but Neala guessed it wasn't so common for a young girl to be asking for them.

"What kind of weapon were you looking for little lady?" he asked, with more sarcasm in his voice than Neala could take.

Swallowing her anger, knowing this man was probably her only chance of replacing her lost weapons any time in the near future, she replied coolly, "I was looking to purchase a set of throwing knives, but only if the quality of your weapons meet my high standards."

The blacksmith's face turned red with anger at her intended insult, and with an extreme look of contempt in his eyes he spat back, "I make the best weapons in Helveel, and probably all of Afaraon, and I only sell them to people capable of wielding them with enough skill, not silly little girls like you!"

Deciding she would rather wait for her knives forever than take any more insults from this man, Neala looked straight at him, and with as much venom in her voice as she could muster replied, "If you call me a little girl again, I'll show you just how much skill I *do* have, and kill you where you stand."

The blacksmith removed his hand from behind his apron and revealed he was carrying a wicked looking knife. Dropping his hammer he lunged towards Neala's throat with his weapon. Neala had already removed her daggers and intercepted his attack with blinding speed and accuracy, parrying his attack harmlessly to the side. Faster and faster they acted and reacted to each other's attacks, neither gaining the upper hand. Neala was impressed with the man's skill level. Apart from her old guild leader, she had never seen anyone as skilful with a weapon as this blacksmith. Together they danced a deadly waltz in the middle of his shop, until Neala saw an opening, and took it. Disarming him of his knife, her dagger came swiftly to his throat. As she looked into his eyes expecting to see fear, she only saw amusement instead. The blacksmith suddenly started laughing at her. Neala was so incensed by him, she was about to end him, when he casually said, "Very good. Looks like you do have a small amount of skill after all. Seems I was wrong about you."

"Some skill? Looks like you're a dead man to me," Neala replied, with her dagger still pressed against his neck.

"I wouldn't be so sure of that if I were you," the blacksmith replied, as he applied a little pressure to a dagger Neala had failed to see, now pressed against her ribcage ready to pierce her heart. *Damn! This guy is good*, she thought to herself.

"So, are you going to sell me some knives or

not?"

The Blacksmith roared with laughter at her casual remark, before lowering his dagger and taking a step back out of harm's way.

"You must be new in these parts. Which guild do belong to?" he asked, putting his weapons away behind his apron, and then retrieving his hammer from the floor.

"I'm not part of any guild. I approached one when I first arrived in Helveel and they refused to take me. They thought I might be a spy I guess. I didn't think it would be too healthy to approach a second guild."

"Smart as well. I like you, girl. Looks like they missed an opportunity to gain a skilled fighter by refusing you entry to their guild," he replied, still smiling at her. Neala got the impression his last statement was as close to a compliment as the man had ever given, and she nodded her approval. "Come, let's go see what we can do about these knives of yours. My workshop is in the back," he said, pointing towards the door he had first emerged through.

Neala followed him into the back of the shop, and was quite surprised at how much larger this area was compared with the part of the shop she had first entered from the street. There were two huge open doors leading out to what looked like a small private courtyard. Two forges stood in the centre of the room—both equipped with bellows, and chimneys that disappeared up through the high roof—and various containers of water, which must have been used for cooling the metal after it came out of the forges. Looking towards the back of the workshop, Neala noticed the whole wall was covered in all manner of weaponry. There were weapons of all shapes and sizes: sword, maces, axes, halberds, pikes, daggers and many other deadly looking items she didn't even know the names of. Slightly startling her from her thoughts regarding all the weapons, the blacksmith asked, "So, what kind of knives were you looking for?"

"Er … I was looking for a price on a set of throwing knives, and a leather belt to hold them, if that's something you can do as well?" she replied, still glancing between him and the huge collection of weapons hanging on the wall.

"Well, for a standard set of six knives I charge two gold. I have a local leather worker who crafts the belts for another two silver. I can have them made in three days time for you, along with the belt. I would need one gold as a deposit before I start to make them however."

Neala was quite shocked at the cost of creating a set of throwing knives, and thought of how foolish she would look when she informed him that she couldn't afford his services after all. She had never bought any weapons for herself in the past. They had always been provided for her by one of the blacksmith shops owned by her guild. Seeing her hesitation, the blacksmith added, "I can assure you, my weapons are of the finest quality, and made from the highest grades of metal money can buy."

Now feeling a little foolish at not asking the price when she first entered the shop, she quietly replied, "Yes, I'm sure the quality of your weapons are second to none, but unfortunately, I only have one gold at present. I apologise for wasting your time sir." Looking away from the blacksmith and waiting for his angry reply, she was surprised to only hear a good humoured laugh instead.

"I might still be able to help you. There's a reason I take a one gold deposit on such items. The kind of work carried out by the people who order such weapons can be, dangerous, as I'm sure you already know. They don't always come back to collect what they have ordered, as you can see from my wall over there," he said, pointing towards the large assortment of weapons. "I do have a set of six throwing knives that were ordered around two months ago now. The man that ordered them has never been back to pay the balance and collect his weapons. I always inform my customers that I'll only keep them for one month after making them. After that they get sold or smelted back into raw materials, and they lose their deposit. If they aren't happy about that, they can always come back and … *discuss* it with me, if they choose," he said grinning at Neala.

Neala had no doubts about how that

conversation would resolve itself, and she was very sure no refunds would be forthcoming.

"The knives were ordered to his specifications. If you're willing to live with that I can let you have them for your one gold. You wanna take a look at them?"

"Yeah, sure. Thanks," Neala replied, not believing her luck. The blacksmith walked over to a large table near the back of the shop and sorted through a pile of items, before returning with the set of throwing knives, and handing it to Neala. She took the belt from him and walked over to an empty table, where she could better inspect the knives.

The first thing she noticed was the belt. It was skilfully made and very robust looking. It was a little heavier than the one she used to own, but that was probably because they were made for a time when she was a little younger. The knives were also very skilfully crafted, and much better quality than her old ones, but again, they were larger and heavier. They were made from one solid piece of steel, and the handles had been drilled to balance them. Lifting and twirling them in her hand, she noticed they weren't entirely balanced correctly. Confused as to why such a well-made knife wouldn't be balanced correctly, she said, "These knives are certainly very well-made, but I noticed the balance isn't quite right on them."

"I see you also know your weapons well," he replied, nodding at her keen observation. "You're correct. The knives are not perfectly balanced. The man who ordered the weapons favoured a slightly heavier handle. The reason he preferred them that way, is only known to him I'm afraid. Like I said, if you're willing to live with his specifications, they're yours for only one gold."

Neala couldn't deny the quality of the weapons in front of her, nor could she afford to buy a newly crafted set to her own specifications from him, or probably anyone else for that matter. After thinking about the various options available to her, which were definitely limited given her current funds, she decided to go out on a limb, and said, "Okay, I'll take them, on one condition. At that price, you throw in a small metal file, so I can balance them myself. I'm sure you know unbalanced throwing knives aren't going to be at the top of most people's shopping lists, and you could be stuck with them for a long time."

The blacksmith roared with laughter, so loud that it made her jump. "Okay, you have yourself a deal, girl. Looks like you bought yourself a set of throwing knives. Most people who come in here I take an instant dislike to, but you, I like. You have spirit girl. If you ever decide you want to join a guild in Helveel, come and see me first. I know a lot of people. I'm sure I can pull some strings and get you into one of the top guilds here," he said, slapping her on the shoulders, and knocking the wind right out of her.

Picking up her new set of throwing knives she fastened them around her waist. The belt was wide and comfortable, and she doubted she would have to make any alterations to it. She accepted the small file and bid him farewell, before returning to the front of the shop and exiting back out onto the cobbled street. The comforting weight at her waist made her feel like she was fully dressed again, for the first time in a long time.

Neala decided to buy their provisions in the west quarter marketplace, while it was still early enough to get the better quality items. After she'd bought what they needed, she turned and headed towards the north quarter of the city. The journey would take more than twice as long, but she didn't want to go back through the west quarter alone again.

The journey back to the shop was long and uneventful. Although Neala was almost sure no one was actually following her, and it was all just in her head, she still fell back on her years of training, and took a route back to the book shop that would lose any potential pursuers. She entered several shops that she knew had more than one exit, switching streets and alleys as she left each one, entering via one door, and quickly exiting through another. Staying within crowds wherever possible, and making it almost impossible to follow her path back to the book shop. When she finally arrived at the street where the book shop was located, she quickly checked that no one would see her entering the shop, before opening the door and slipping inside, she then swiftly closed the door behind herself.

The shop area was empty, so she called out to the back of the shop to inform them it was only her entering, and so there was no need to come through to serve any potential customers. She thought she heard a reply, and continued downstairs to meet up with Lusam again.

Entering the book room she almost walked straight into a large pile of books floating through the air towards where Lusam was standing.

"I've got us some breakfast," Neala said, holding out a sweet pastry wrapped in brown paper and an apple.

"Mm-mm … thanks, I'm starving. I don't know why, but doing magic always makes me feel ravenous," he said. Lusam took the two items from Neala, opened the packet containing the sweet pastry and completely wolfed it down, even before Neala had opened hers.

"I think I'd better start buying you more food if

you're going to eat it that fast," Neala said laughing at Lusam's face, which now had sticky fruit sauce all around his mouth.

"Sorry," he replied, trying to clean around his mouth with his tongue. "Did you manage to find what you were looking for?"

"Yes, kind of. I got a set of throwing knives, but I'll have to balance them myself. It's a long story," she replied, before filling him in on all the details. Lusam looked quite worried when she recounted the part of the story where she had fought the blacksmith, but he didn't comment on it.

"Sounds like you had some fun this morning," Lusam said, still trying to get every last bit of the apple from its core.

"Yeah, nothing like an early morning workout," she replied laughing. Neala decided not to tell him about the strange feelings of being followed, in case he thought she was just being paranoid. "How's it going with the books? Seems you have a large stack to sort through at the moment," Neala said, trying to change the subject.

"It's going much faster now that I can move large numbers of books with my magic. I guess we don't need that wheelbarrow anymore," he replied. "It should be a lot easier on our backs from now on too."

"If you don't need me to move books for the time being, would you mind if I start balancing these knives?" Neala asked hopefully.

"No problem at all," replied Lusam. He was happy that she would have something to occupy herself with, while he continued cataloguing the books.

"Do you have any of that chalk left you used on the walls?" Neala asked.

"Yeah. There are a couple of sticks of it here. How many do you need?"

"Oh, just one is fine thanks. I found an old table in one of the rooms a while back. I was planning to take it into the large room. I figured that if I stood it up against the wall, and drew some targets on it with the chalk, it would help me balance my knives."

Lusam found the chalk and handed a stick to Neala. "There's more if you need it. Do you need a hand with that old table?" he asked.

"Thanks, but it didn't look very heavy. Besides, I doubt it matters if I damage it slightly by dragging it around if I'm going to be throwing knives at it anyway," she said laughing.

"True, I guess," he agreed laughing along with her. "If you do need any help, just let me know."

"Okay, thanks. I think I'll eat my breakfast first, then go get the table," she said, finding a seat on a pile of books and opening her own sweet pastry. Noticing Lusam hungrily eyeing up her breakfast, she just laughed and tossed her apple to him. "Here, eat this. I'm not that hungry at the moment, and I can't train on a full stomach anyway." Lusam deftly caught the apple in mid-flight, smiled at her, and started munching on the juicy apple. Neala just smiled at him, shaking her head ever so slightly to herself, and continued eating her pastry.

Later that morning Neala managed to move the old table into the main chamber. She removed the legs from the table quite easily. In fact, it almost removed its own legs, as it stood swaying from side to side. It looked like the old wood had dried out completely, and the joints had become very loose. It had been a simple task of pushing it to one side, and the legs had just folded under the table with the sideways pressure. She was now left with a large board: which had once been the table top. It was about the same height as her when she stood it up against the wall, and maybe twice as wide as a person. For a few moments Neala wondered what type of target to draw on the large board, before deciding it might as well be human-shaped. Standing with her back to the board, she traced, as best she could, around her own body with the chalk onto the table top, switching hands with the chalk several times in the process.

When she had finished she took a few steps back and looked at the outline. '*Not bad*,' she thought to herself. A few minutes spent on strengthening the lines and smoothing parts out, and she was left with an accurate outline of a person of average height. She added a few targets within the outline to represent various kill points, before moving back ten paces to have a go at throwing a knife at the target. She knew the knives were not balanced, but decided to see how they would fly anyway. It didn't take Neala long to realise they were a long way from perfect for her. Over half of them hit the target handle first, which for obvious reasons, wouldn't be much good in a fight of life and death. Neala knew she could adapt to them eventually, but that meant almost having to relearn the skill of throwing knives all over again; something she wasn't prepared to do. An advantage of centre-balanced knives was the fact you could throw them accurately from either the handle or blade, something you couldn't do with an unbalanced knife. If you trained to throw balanced knives, you could throw any balanced knife accurately. If you normally used unbalanced knives, you would have to learn each knife set individually, which could be a big disadvantage, especially if you happen to have just picked up a random knife during a fight, only to find out you couldn't throw it accurately.

Thinking about the knives, her best guess was

that the man who had originally ordered them, had been taught to throw using an unbalanced set, and therefore he would always order them that way if he could, to maintain his accuracy. Neala knew she preferred them balanced, and so, she started the long process of filing the handles of each knife to achieve a perfect balance point. It was hard work, and she estimated she was only about half-way through balancing the first knife, when Lusam came into the room and announced he was hungry again. Rolling her eyes, she pointed towards the package of food near the door, before continuing to file her knife handle.

"That looks like a laborious job," Lusam said, nodding towards the knife and file in her hands.

"No kidding. The metal that blacksmith used is very good quality, but it makes it incredibly difficult to file anything off, because it's so hard," Neala replied, slightly out of breath and sweating.

"Can I take a look?" Lusam asked, holding out his hand. Neala handed him the knife, and then watched as he inspected the file-work she had already done on the handle. "How much more do you think you need to take off?"

"I'm not sure. Maybe about the amount same again. I prefer the handle and blade to be perfectly balanced at the half way point, or as close as possible," she replied, pointing to the centre of another knife.

"I see," he replied, studying the knife carefully. "I noticed you're filing off the weight from the handle. Would it make any difference if the blade was slightly longer, and the handle equally slightly shorter?"

"No, not really. I'm making the handle shorter anyway by filing it. Balance is the most important thing for a throwing knife. Why do you ask?"

"Well … remember when I made those gold coins? I think I could do something similar with your knives. I could put them in a force-field, heat them up, and lengthen the blades slightly. Metal from the handle would be added to the blade section as I manipulate the force-field," he replied, with a thoughtful look on his face.

"Really? You could do that?" Neala asked, a little shocked at his suggestion.

"I guess there's only one way to find out, but they're your knives, so you have to decide whether to take the gamble or not." Thinking for a moment longer, he added, "Worst case scenario; I mess them up, and you'd have to wait a few days until Seventh-day, until I could make a few more gold coins. Then you could simply go back and buy some balanced knives from that blacksmith. As long as you don't kill him this time," he said, laughing at his own joke.

"Hey!" she said, slapping his arm. As she hit his arm he dropped the sharp knife, and it sank deep into his foot. Lusam screamed with the sudden pain in his foot, stumbled backwards, and found himself sitting on the floor staring open mouthed at the knife protruding from his foot.

"Oh gods! I'm so sorry Lusam," Neala said, panicking at the sight of her knife in Lusam's foot. "What shall I do? Shall I go get the healer to come down here? Oh, I'm so, so sorry!" Neala was almost beside herself with grief at what she had done to

Lusam.

Breathing through the pain, Lusam replied, "It's okay, just wait a second." He concentrated on the area of his foot where the knife was sticking out, and searching his, newly acquired, knowledge of healing magic, he applied a spell to stop the pain emanating from it. With a huge sigh of relief, he lay back on the floor. He then took several deep breaths, desperately trying to stop himself from feeling so nauseous. Now that his mind was free of the pain, he could think much more clearly for a solution to his predicament. He realised the book had taught him how to heal wounds, and although he was confident he could complete the spell successfully, he would have preferred his first attempt had not been on himself.

"Neala, I need you to pull out the knife," he said, still lying flat on his back. "If I do it myself, I think I'll just throw up."

"But, if I pull it out it's going to hurt you even more. I've already hurt you enough," she replied almost in tears.

"No. Don't worry, it won't hurt me. I've already

blocked the pain with magic. I definitely need you to remove the knife though. I've never been good with blood, especially my own," he replied, still looking at the ceiling.

"Okay ... if you're sure you want me to do that?" she asked, looking at his very pale and sweaty face. He nodded his agreement to her, so she quickly bent down, and removed the knife in one swift movement. Much to her relief, Lusam didn't make a sound, but now she was stood holding one of her knives, coated in her best friend's blood. She had seen blood many more times than she cared to remember, but never had it effected her this way. Putting the knife down, she went to Lusam's side and took hold of his hand. Lusam looked up at Neala and smiled at her, then squeezed her hand.

"Don't worry. I'll be fine," he tried to reassure her. "Could you remove my boot please? I'm not sure I can sit up yet, and it feels like it's bleeding quite badly. I can feel my boot filling up."

At that Neala began to look even more worried, but she began to loosen his boot as he asked. When she was able to remove the boot and see the wound for herself, she was amazed how calm Lusam was. The knife had passed right through his foot, and left a nasty looking hole the full width of the blade. His boot did indeed contain a lot of blood—as he had said—but far more concerning, was the amount of blood now flowing freely from his foot. The knife must have cut through a blood vessel of some kind, and now it was pumping from his foot with each beat of his heart.

Lusam concentrated on his foot with his mage-sight, and applied his new healing knowledge to the wound. First he had to reconnect the severed dorsalis pedis artery, which was responsible for pumping out the blood so fast. How he even knew the name of it was a mystery, but one he would ponder over at a more appropriate time. Bringing the two severed parts together, he fused them back into one piece with magic, before moving on to inspect the rest of the injury. He didn't find anything else too serious, and began knitting the wound back together from the inside out. When he reached the surface layer, he pulled the two sides of skin back together, before finally sealing the wound completely.

When he opened his eyes he saw Neala still staring at his foot with her mouth wide open, as if in mid-sentence. She noticed Lusam looking up at her, and still completely speechless, she simply shook her head, before almost diving on top of him, and enveloping him with a huge hug.

"That was amazing! Your wound just healed right before my eyes. How did you do that?" she asked in a shaky voice.

"It was amongst the spells I learned from the book, fortunately for me. I was hoping to try it out on someone else first, though, to be honest." Tentatively he removed the spell suppressing the pain, and was relieved to find he no longer had any pain in his foot. He wiggled his toes and rotated his ankle to make doubly sure everything was working correctly, then with a sigh, he said, "I suppose I better go wash all of the blood out of my boot before I put it back on again."

"Oh, no you don't! I'll go do that for you. It's

the least I can do after causing the problem in the first place," she said, reaching for his boot. "You stay right here and eat your lunch. I'll be right back."

Lusam almost lost control of his stomach at the thought of eating anything. "I think I'll give food a wide berth for a little while," he replied, still looking very pale.

Neala took the boot and disappeared up the stairs towards the shop above. After a few minutes Lusam began to feel much better, and sat upright to look around the room. He noticed the knife on the floor that had been inside his foot only a few minutes earlier. Reaching over, he picked it up to take a closer look at it. He was no expert when it came to knives, although, he could testify with absolute conviction at how sharp the blade was, but even he could tell it wasn't well balanced: the handle was much heavier than the blade. He decided to try and correct the balance while Neala was gone. He very much doubted Neala would give him a hard time, even if he did end up destroying the knife whilst trying to correct its balance. Not after what had just happened.

193

He formed a close fitting force-field around the knife, and began to heat the metal. Once it was molten, he simultaneously lengthened the blade, whilst reducing the length of the handle. He carefully reached out his hand towards the force-field, not knowing if the still molten metal inside would effect the temperature of the outside of the force-field. He was almost touching the force-field, but he couldn't feel any heat emanating from it, so he made brief contact with it to be sure. The force-field was as cool as stone to his touch, so he released the levitation spell and let it fall gently into his hand. Finding the half way point of the knife, he adjusted the length of the blade and handle, until it was perfectly balanced on his finger. Once he was happy with the shape and balance, he rapidly reduced the temperature inside the force-field to cool the metal. When he was certain it was cool enough, he released the force-field, letting the new knife settle into the palm of his hand.

After carefully inspecting the new knife, he was pleased with the results, and hoped Neala would be equally pleased. Almost as an after thought, he decided to add a small enchantment to the knife. It would strengthen the metal further, and keep the blade sharp and free from corrosion; no matter what.

He was keen to see how sharp the knife was, and spotted the food parcel over near the door. He hobbled over to the door wearing only one boot, noticing how warm the stone floor was on his bare foot. He picked up a piece of brown paper packaging, and tried the knife against its edge. The knife cut through the paper like a razor blade. Happy with the results, he looked around for more things to test it on, but there was nothing else around. He was just about to hobble back to the book room to await Neala's return, when he noticed the new target that she had made from the old table.

"How hard can it be?" he said out loud to himself, hobbling towards the target. He quickly decided that he didn't want to be too close, just in case the knife bounced back at him; one injury was more than enough for one day. Moving back another ten paces, he turned to face the target. Should he hold the blade or the handle? He had no idea. Settling for holding the blade, he took aim and threw the knife fairly hard at the target, giving it every chance to stick into the wood. He watched the knife fly through the air and miss the wooden target by a small margin. Cringing as the knife was about to smash into the hard stone wall. He thought he might have to quickly repair or remake the knife before Neala returned, especially if his enchantment didn't work to protect it.

As the knife was about to strike the stone wall, a huge red flash radiated outwards from the impact, before dissipating all around the room. Lusam stood there staring at the wall, as if expecting it to do something else, but it remained just a wall. He looked at the wall using his mage-sight, and was shocked to see that the text carved into the wall, now glowed like the pressure points they had found outside the secret room. He still couldn't read the strange language the words were written in, however. As Lusam looked around the room, he noticed other inscriptions carved into the walls, all glowing brightly in his mage-sight, and also a few high above him on the vaulted ceiling. He remembered seeing some kind of pictures depicted up there when they had first arrived, but it had never been light enough to see what they were pictures of.

Returning to his normal-sight, Lusam created a light orb and sent it up towards the ceiling, curious as to what was above him. He increased its light level as it went up, and revealed the most amazing sight he had ever seen. Huge pictures of what looked like both dragons and men, standing together, next to the immense building and towers of some ancient long forgotten temple. In two of the pictures, the dragons had what looked like human riders on their backs. In others, it showed what appeared to be men and women cleaning and feeding them. One building in the picture grabbed Lusam's attention more than any other. It was a large domed-topped building with glowing red walls. It showed three figures standing in front of the building, each one casting what looked like magical missiles towards the walls of the building. When he studied it further, he noticed that although it looked like they were standing outside the building, in fact, they were actually inside, and the artist had just removed the front walls to reveal the interior for the benefit of the picture.

Lusam let the light orb wink out high up above him. He stared back at the walls surrounding him, while thinking about what he had just seen. Were these walls like the ones in the picture above his head? What would be the point of magically protecting the inside of a building, when attacks would come from outside? None of it made any sense to him. Then with sudden realisation it came to him. These walls weren't built to protect the monks from outside attackers, they were made to absorb magic, so they could train here without damaging the building itself.

Keen to test his theory, he was equally keen not to bring the roof down on top of his head, and so, decided to start off with only very weak basic spells. He chose a fire based spell, and sent a weak fireball towards the wall from a safe distance. As soon as the fireball made contact with the wall, the same red shimmer flashed around the room, dissipating the effects of the fireball. Lusam could see there were no visible marks on the wall where the fireball should have hit, so he increased the power of his spell, and sent another fireball towards the wall. This time the red flare was more intense, but still, there was no damage to the wall. He tried several more times, each time increasing the power of the fireballs he sent, and each time the walls flashed red and dispelled the effects.

Lusam was about to try other spells, when Neala returned to the room carrying a clean, but very wet looking boot. Handing the dripping boot back to Lusam, he took it and said, "Er ... thanks ... I think."

"Sorry it's so wet, it took a while to get all the blood out of it. I thought you might be able to dry it with your magic," she replied apologetically.

Searching his mind for an appropriate spell to dry his boot, he realised he didn't have one. "Actually, I don't know how," he said, laughing at the crazy thought of being able to create gold coins and weapons, or bring down a building with a simple thought, but not being able to dry his own boot. "I guess I still have a lot to learn."

"You're looking much better anyway," Neala offered in a low voice.

"Yeah, I'm fine, don't worry. While you were gone I altered your knife for you. It seems to have worked out quite well, but I'm no expert, you'll have to tell me what you think before I do the others. I also placed a magical enchantment on the knife, so it should be much stronger than before, and never need sharpening or oiling for rust protection," he said, walking over to retrieve the knife, which was still on the floor near the target board. He picked up the knife, walked back to where Neala was standing, and handed it to her carefully. She twirled the knife in her hand, and flipped it over in mid-air a couple of times, before sending it flying towards the target board. With a thud, the knife struck dead centre of the heart shaped target.

"Perfectly balanced! Thanks Lusam," Neala said, throwing her arms around his neck and giving him another big hug, as well as a kiss on the cheek.

"Great, I'm glad you like it. Five more knives to balance and enchant then. Does that mean I'll get five more hugs and kisses when I'm done?" Lusam asked, trying to keep a serious look on his face. Neala just smiled and winked at him, before going to retrieve her new knife.

"I've found a couple of very interesting things while you were gone too," Lusam said, walking back to the area directly under the picture on the vaulted ceiling.

"Oh?" Neala replied curiously.

"Do you remember when we first arrived here, I noticed some paintings high up above where I'm standing now, but we couldn't see them because it was too dark?"

"I didn't see them, but I remember you telling me you saw something up there. Why do you ask?" Neala replied, walking over to where Lusam was now standing.

"Take a look for yourself. See what you think," Lusam replied.

A light orb suddenly appeared high above him—illuminating the ceiling—and revealed the full splendour of the incredibly detailed artwork that had been previously hidden by the darkness. He heard Neala take a sudden intake of breath, as the whole image became visible.

"That's amazing! It must have taken years to paint all of that," she said in a whisper, almost as if she was afraid that one of the painted figures would overhear her comments.

"Yeah, I bet they had sore necks too," Lusam laughed. "But, the part I wanted to show you is there on the left. That building in front of those mountains. The one with the domed roof and red walls. Can you see it?"

"Er … oh, yes, I see it. It looks like it's under attack by those figures in front of it," Neala replied, still overawed by the sheer size and scale of the painted ceiling.

"Yes, that's the one. I thought it was under attack too when I first saw it. But if you look closer, what looks like the outside wall of the building, is actually the interior wall. The artist has simply removed the front wall, so we're able to see inside the building," he said, trying to point out the small, but obvious details.

"Yes, I think you're right. But why would anyone attack the inside of a building like that?" Neala asked, confused.

"Again, I thought the same thing when I first saw it, but it's not what it seems," he said, extinguishing the light above them. "Come over here, I'll show you." And he walked back to where he first discovered the walls innate ability to absorb impacts and magic. "Throw one of you knives at your target, but I want you to miss and hit the wall instead."

Neala looked at him as if he had gone mad. "But, if I hit the wall instead of the target, it would likely destroy my knife. Or at the very least, it would need a lot of attention afterwards."

"Well … it doesn't really matter that much anyway. I'll be changing them with magic when I balance them for you, but I doubt it will be damaged in any case. Trust me," he said, smiling at her.

Still not convinced by his logic, she decided not to argue, and just throw the knife like he'd asked. It took a surprising amount of self control for Neala to ignore the fact, that her new knife would probably be badly damaged after deliberately hitting a solid stone wall, but she put her natural instincts aside, and let the knife fly towards its fate. Just as the knife was about to hit the stone wall, a red flash erupted from the impact site, then dissipated outwards along the walls around the room.

"Wow! What was that?" Neala blurted out.

"I think that was the same thing we just saw in the picture on the ceiling," Lusam replied, pointing up at where the pictures now lay in darkness. "I think this huge room was used by the monks who lived here to practise magic, and maybe other offensive skills. The walls seem to absorb the impact of anything that hits them. I suppose it makes sense really, when you think about it. If you need to practise potentially dangerous magic, you couldn't really do it out on the streets, or even out in the open air safely. Eventually it would hit something, and damage or destroy it, or even kill someone. Watch I'll show you," Lusam said, turning around and sending a fireball hurtling towards the wall. As before the impact was completely dissipated by the wall.

"Wow! This place gets stranger every day," Neala said, shaking her head.

Laughing, Lusam replied, "Yeah, I agree. It would also explain why the walls and floor are always warm in winter and cool in summer. It's because they are magical in nature." Neala just nodded her head, still trying to take in the strangeness of it all. "Looks like we will both be practising in here from now on in our spare time," Lusam said, looking around the huge room.

"Practising?" Neala asked confused.

"Yeah. While you practise your knife throwing, I can practise what I learnt from the book. Some of the spells are a little confusing, and other are very complicated. This place seems like the perfect place to get some practice and increase my skills, with no chance of damaging anything accidentally, or being seen by anyone."

Neala thought for a moment, then grinning widely, she replied, "That sounds like a good idea. But, I think I'll stay out of your way while you're throwing magic around in here. If you don't mind, that is? I wouldn't want to find myself suddenly faced with a stray fireball, or worse. Even if you do owe me one for that foot of yours."

Lusam burst out laughing at the image that popped into his mind, of Neala being chased around the huge room by a stray fireball with a mind of its own.

"Sure, no problem. I can always practise after you're done," he suggested.

"Yeah, that sounds somewhat … safer to me," Neala said, laughing back at his sudden outburst. Thinking to herself for a few moments, she added, "I do have a question though. That fireball you just sent at the wall, could you create a smaller version, or something similar to cook food with? If you could, it would vastly increase the choice of food I'm able to buy."

"Hmm … I never thought about that," he said running the possibility through his mind. "Yes, I believe I could. I could even levitate the food above the fire, so we wouldn't need any cooking implements. And if I placed a small force-field below the fire, any food drips wouldn't make a mess on the floor either," he replied, feeling very pleased with himself. Suddenly, images of a slow-turning roast pig, levitating above a magical fire sprang into his mind, loudly awakening his stomach to the fact that he hadn't eaten since this morning. He was about to inform Neala, when she broke the silence.

"I know … I know … you're hungry. Again," she said, rolling her eyes and going over to retrieve their lunch from near the doorway. Lusam just smiled to himself, content in the knowledge that she knew him so well.

After lunch Lusam found himself still hungry, as usual. Nothing seemed to fill him these days since he'd started doing more magic, or if it did, not for long. He spent the next hour adjusting Neala's knives using his magic, which only made him even more hungry, before returning to his book duties. Neala spent the afternoon familiarising herself with her new weapons in the large room, practising on her wooden target board. In the beginning, the constant thud ... thud ... thud of the knives hitting the wooden board, almost drove him to distraction. But after a couple of hours, it became an almost comforting background noise. He knew Neala was happy in there practising, and so, that made him happy too.

Later that evening, after Neala's reading lesson, Lusam returned to the large room and started practising his various new spells alone. Each day over the next few weeks followed a very similar pattern. The only difference was he got much better at casting his spells, and the size of the book mountain reduced substantially; to the point they both could see an end in sight.

Spring had definitely now arrived in Afaraon. The days were becoming warmer and longer, and the birds that migrated there for the summer months were now often seen in the sky above. On each Seventh-day they could now spend much more time filtering the river of its precious gold, which meant they had started to collect quite a princely sum together.

Lusam had been worried about getting the exact

design of the gold coins right, just in case someone became suspicious and started to investigate the source of the strange coins. For the past two days, he had asked Neala to buy their food in the richer northern quarter of town, using their gold coins. Then, after the second day, he had collected enough silver coins together from the change, to exchange for a genuine gold coin at the bank. From that coin, he would copy the design for all his future coins; therefore, there would be no way to tell they weren't actually genuine minted coins.

Each time they spent a day by the side of the river, they usually managed to make between three and four coins, depending on how far up or down river they ventured. These gold coins, added to the silver coins they had earned from Mr Daffer, meant that they would have more than enough to last them for a long while after they had finished the job at the book shop.

From the start, Lusam and Neala had kept their gold and silver coins safe in one of the small wooden chests that were to be found in most of the sleeping cells. However, Lusam realised that when they finally finished the job for Mr Daffer, and they left the underground chamber for good, they wouldn't be able to carry a wooden chest around with them on the streets of Helveel, for obvious reasons. With this in mind, they had visited the local leather workers shop and bought two coin pouches, which could be concealed under their tunics out of sight. The craftsman had also suggested that he should add a metal wire inside the string of the coin pouch, making it almost impossible for a cut-purse to steal it by the usual methods, should it be spotted under their garments. Neala's coin pouch fastened easily to her thick knife belt, but Lusam's kept trying to pull down his trousers with the weight of the coins, and he was forced to return to the leather shop the following day to purchase a belt for himself; to avoid any future potentially embarrassing moments.

Lusam lay on his bed smiling contently to himself. He was absent-mindedly staring at the ceiling of his sleeping cell, day-dreaming, and thinking of his past, and possible future. Life was good at the moment for Lusam. It had been a long time since he'd felt so relaxed, and in control of his own life. He no longer had to look forward to only a hard life on the streets, without food, shelter or warmth. He could easily provide enough coin for the rest of his life. He also no longer had to worry about being attacked on the streets on Helveel, by anyone who wanted what he had.

Lusam's mind wandered freely, and eventually he found himself thinking about Neala, and what she might want to do after leaving Mr Daffer's shop. He thought about where they might go together, and what they might do there. Suddenly, he got a knot in his stomach. He realised, that even after spending all that time together, not once, had they ever discussed what they would do when they left the book shop. For all Lusam knew, Neala might want to go her own separate way, now that she had plenty of her own money, and set up life in another part of the country. Alone. That thought hit him like a thunderbolt. He sat up from his bed, almost breathless with panic at the thought of losing Neala. He knew in that instant he loved her beyond doubt, but he had no idea if she felt the same way about him. He could not even imagine losing her, nor did he want to try.

Lusam sat on the edge of his bed, trying to think of a way to ask Neala how she felt about him, and what she planned to do in the very near future, when they were finally finished at the book shop. He couldn't believe how nervous he was just thinking about discussing the subject with Neala, just in case he didn't like what she said, but he knew he must talk with her, and soon. Very soon. Standing up from his bed, he left his room, and headed to where Neala slept.

Lusam could see the gentle light of a lantern spilling from her room into the dark corridor up ahead, and was overtaken by a fresh wave of nervousness, as he realised she was still awake. He knew there would be no possibility he could sleep anyway if he didn't speak to her now, so he continued down the dark corridor until he came to her door.

"Neala … are you still awake?" he said, in a

soft voice from the corridor.

Neala was reading one of the books Lusam had used to teach her how to read when she heard Lusam call softly from outside her door. "Yes, come in," she replied, through the open door.

Lusam took a deep breath to steady his nerves, before walking through the door and into the light of Neala's room.

"Is everything alright?" Neala asked, looking concerned at his late visit, and the worried look on Lusam's face.

"Yes. Yes, I hope so …" he replied, sounding a little unsure of himself.

Placing her book on the bed Neala stood up and approached Lusam. "So, are you going to tell me?" she asked, smiling at him.

Sometimes, Lusam was sure that Neala knew exactly what he was going to say, even before he said it, and only wanted to torture him, by making him say it out loud. Swallowing any pretence at bravery, he decided to just say what was on his mind.

"Well … as you know, in the next couple of

days we should be finished here … "

"Yes?" she prompted.

"Well … I was, er … wondering, if you had given any thought to what you might do after we leave here," he said, gesturing around with his hands.

"I'm not sure I know what you mean?" she replied, still wearing that smile of hers. Lusam was sure she knew exactly what he meant, and was just taking great pleasure in making him squirm so much, as he tiptoed around the real issue.

"I was in my room just now, thinking about what we would do when we leave here, and I realised, we've never spoken about it before," he said, looking more worried by the second.

Neala took a step closer to Lusam, and looked up into his eyes. "Not so long ago, a handsome young man told me that we were a team. I hope he hasn't changed his mind," she half whispered to him, looking deep into his eyes. Lusam almost rocked as his mind tried to take in the full meaning of her words.

"Neala … I … I love you," he whispered back,

hoping beyond hope that he hadn't misread her words, or her body language.

"I love you too," she replied, throwing her arms around his neck, and embracing him tightly.

Those few words were the best sounds Lusam had ever heard in his whole life. The sudden relief that washed over him, almost made him feel dizzy. She actually loved him too!

Life just couldn't get any better than this, he thought. Feeling wet on his neck, he realised Neala was crying. Pulling away slightly to get a better look at her face, he asked, "What's the matter? Are you okay?"

Smiling at him through tears of joy, she just nodded her head, then kissed him, like he'd never been kissed before.

Chapter Seven

As they came within sight of Helveel the heavens opened, and another heavy spring downpour drenched the two men. Already wearied by their long trip from Stelgad, and wanting nothing more than to find a warm inn that served good ale and a bed for the night; the weather did little to improve their mood. Travelling the long road between Stelgad and Helveel at this time of year, was at best unpleasant, but could easily be deadly for any unwary travellers. The main road skirted the southern Elveen mountains, and at this time of year, that usually meant warm but very wet days, followed by freezing temperatures at night. With only two horses and no covered wagon to travel in, that meant their clothes were constantly wet to the skin, never having time to dry, before the cold air from the mountains tried to freeze them to death each night.

Both men had agreed many times on their journey, that whoever was responsible for them having to make this godforsaken trip, would pay dearly before they handed them over to their boss Shiva. Skelly would have liked nothing better than to simply kill whoever they had been sent to find, but his orders were clear. He had been instructed in no uncertain terms, that he must return the culprit alive, and unharmed for Shiva to deal with personally. Even Skelly dare not cross Shiva, but he was a skilled assassin, and could inflict more than enough pain without leaving any evidence behind, and he planned to do just that.

They entered Helveel via the south gate, then headed directly through the city to the northern quarter. One thing Skelly was well known for, was his love of the finer things in life, and he wasn't concerned how much they cost, as long as they met with his strict high standards. Skelly was accepted within his guild as being the unofficial second in command, with only Shiva above him in the chain of command. Being in such a position brought many advantages, including among other things, a plentiful supply of coin.

Entering the northern quarter Skelly briefly stopped his horse, and asked a well dressed man for his recommendation of an inn. He was directed two streets further north, where he was told he would find an excellent establishment called the *Golden Feather.*

Sure enough, when they arrived they found a well cared for building, with fresh flowers in hanging baskets outside, and the irresistible smell of fine food coming from the kitchens around the back. Noticing them stop at the front of the building, a young stable boy came to greet them, and offered to take their horses for feeding and grooming. Skelly nodded his approval and flipped a silver coin to the young lad, then both men headed inside to procure rooms and refreshments.

Skelly had chosen Carter to accompany him on

this trip for mainly one reason. He was the only other member of his guild, that he knew of, who also appreciated the higher class establishments, and more importantly, knew how to act within them. Bringing anyone else from his guild to a place like this, would have inevitably resulted in a brawl, with them both being ejected, or possibly arrested by the town guards before the end of the night. The others were far more used to sawdust and blood on the floor, than polished wood and carpets. And, although Skelly was happy to rough it with the rest, given a choice, this would always be his first preference.

Both men approached the bar, where a pretty serving girl with long dark hair and brown eyes stood drying a tankard with a clean cloth. She suspiciously watched their approach, but remained where she was.

"Can I help you gentlemen with something?" she asked, in a clear well-spoken voice.

Skelly stepped forward and cleared his throat, "Yes, I hope so Miss. My friend and I are in need of a room each. Preferably with a bath if you have one please. We were also looking to have a meal if possible?"

The young girl looked surprised at Skelly's well spoken manner, obviously expecting something quite different from the look of him and his dirty travelling clothes. It was apparent to Skelly that she didn't really know how to answer his request, so he attempted to put her a little more at ease by saying, "I'm sorry, how rude of me. My name is Skelly, and my associate here is Carter. You will have to excuse our appearance, we have just arrived in Helveel from Stelgad. It's been a long and hard journey. May I ask if you have a laundry service too? As you can see, our clothes are in desperate need of cleaning after our long journey."

Skelly was an expert at infiltrating the higher classes of society and gaining their trust, which was essential to some of the guilds larger acquisitions. Gaining the respect of this young girl was child's play in comparison to them. Sure enough the girl visibly relaxed, as she readjusted her assessment of the two men standing before her.

"My name is Anna. Pleased to meet you both,"

she replied, looking far more relaxed now. "We do have two rooms available on the second floor, if that would be suitable for your needs?"

"I'm sure they will be just fine, thank you," replied Skelly.

"Very good sir. With regards to your other requests. We do have a bath house here on the ground floor that you may use. Just let myself or one of the others know when you wish to use it, and we will make sure you have plenty of hot water and towels available. I could have your clothes collected from your rooms for washing later this evening when you retire, and have them brought back to you by morning, if that is acceptable? With regards to the food, we serve soup, cold meats and bread throughout the day, and evening meal is available between seven and nine o'clock. Tonight we are serving a choice of either roast beef and vegetables, or grilled river trout and vegetables."

"That sounds wonderful. We will take the two rooms for one night, with a view to extending our stay, depending on how our business here in Helveel goes tomorrow. Please could you also send up two platters of cold meat and bread with some of your finest ale at your earliest convenience?"

"Of course sir. That will be one gold for the two rooms, and two silver for the platter and ale. Would you also like me to reserve you a table for the evening meal?" she asked, while taking two keys off their hooks and placing them on the counter.

"Yes please, if you wouldn't mind. We will be downstairs around seven o'clock, if that's acceptable?" Skelly replied, placing two gold coins on the counter and taking the keys in exchange.

"Yes sir, that's fine. I'll make sure your table is ready for you by seven. If you will excuse me, I shall fetch your change."

"No need. Please, keep the change as a token of our gratitude, for all of your help," Skelly said smiling, and performing a small mock bow towards her.

"Why, thank you sir. That's most generous of you. I hope your stay with us here at the *Golden feather* is a very pleasant one," she replied, returning his mock bow with a similar curtsy of her own, before turning and disappearing into the back room, obviously very happy with her generous tip.

Carter glanced at Skelly with a puzzled look on his face, but knew better than to ask questions here where they could be overheard, so he took one of the keys and they both went to find their rooms. The rooms were adjacent to one another, with a lockable connecting door between the two rooms. As expected, both rooms were impeccably clean, with crisp white bed linens, thick velvet curtains, and various pieces of opulent looking furniture dotted around the room. Carter closed the door behind them, before asking, "What was all that about?"

"All what?" Skelly asked, still inspecting the contents of the room.

"The fake accent. Speaking like you're some lord, and the king-sized tip you left that bar maid," Carter replied, hoping he hadn't overstepped his mark: Skelly wasn't known for his kind nature or small talk.

Skelly turned to look at Carter, who he could

see was instantly regretting asking the question. But after the hard two week journey they had just endured, being here in a warm dry and comfortable inn, with the prospect of some fine food and drink, not to mention a bath, had put Skelly in a good mood for a change. He didn't want to spoil it by killing his travelling companion, and having to go and find another place to stay in a poorer part of the city.

"If you really need to know … someone once told me: '*If you let people think you have nothing, they will keep you with nothing.*' Or in other words, if they think you're worth something, they will treat you as such. As for the tip, that will buy us far more in the way of service and quality of food and ale over the coming night, than the sum I gave her would ever do in reality—you'll see," Skelly replied, studying Carter to see if he truly understood. "Anything else you'd like to know?"

Carter just shook his head nervously, before pointing with his chin towards the adjoining door. "I think I'll go check out my room and wait for the food, leave you to settle in here," he said, quickly heading towards the door without waiting for a reply. Skelly just nodded to himself. At least Carter was smart enough not to bug him too much. He liked him for that. Whether it would be enough if he got under Skelly's skin when he wasn't in such a good mood, was another matter entirely.

The next morning Skelly and Carter headed straight for the horse-trader that had been spotted with their guild horse. They found the horse-trader on the outskirts of the city, in the southern part of Helveel. It looked like whoever had stolen the horse, had sold it to the first trader they had come across in Helveel. As luck would have it, the guild horse was still there in the corral. Plainly visible on its hind quarters, was the guild symbol that was branded on all their livestock in Stelgad. A large man noticed them looking at the horse, and came over to the fence to ask if they were interested in buying the animal.

"Morning good sirs," he said, lifting off his hat a little and bobbing his head. "A fine animal that one. I'm sure we can come to agree a fair price for it, if you're interested."

Neither man responded to the horse-trader, but Skelly turned to stare at him with those cold deadly blue eyes of his, before turning his attention back to the horse. Nodding towards the animal, he asked in a cold voice that would shake the confidence of most men, "Where did you get that horse?"

Looking from one man to the other, the horse-trader gave the impression he didn't intimidate easily. *Too bad for him*, Skelly thought.

"If I have to ask you again, it's going to get painful for you," Skelly said, taking a step closer to the fence that separated him and the horse-trader. The man obviously wasn't used to been spoken to in this manner, and took a step towards the fence in a show of defiance. Skelly approved of his bravery, then baulked at his stupidity. The horse-trader lifted one arm to point down the road, whilst grabbing a fencepost with his other hand.

"Get the hell off my property you … AARGH!" he screamed, as his hand was pinned to the top of the fencepost by Skelly's dagger. Skelly had moved so fast, even Carter hadn't seen what was coming. Skelly's actions took Carter by complete surprise, so much so, he took an involuntary step back as the knife pierced the man's hand. The man stood there whimpering in pain, as his blood flowed down his fingers, dripping onto the grass below. Skelly kept a firm hold of the dagger, and moved closer to the man. He removed a second dagger, then placed it across the horse-trader's little finger, applying a small amount of pressure.

"Okay, I'll ask again. Where did you get that horse?"

"Go to hell … AARGH!" he screamed again, as his little finger fell from his hand to join the rest of his blood on the floor. Moving his dagger to the next finger, Skelly once again applied a little pressure.

"Wrong answer. But, I guess you have nineteen more attempts to get it right. Where did you get the horse?" Skelly asked again. This time his question was met only with a stony silence, until he let out another scream, as a second finger hit the floor. Skelly was genuinely impressed by the horse-trader's guts—but that wouldn't save him if he didn't talk. Again, Skelly moved on to the the next finger, and asked his question once more.

"Where did you get the horse?"

Whimpering through the pain, he heard the man say something.

"Louder, I can't hear you. Or I'll cut off another one."

"A GIRL!" the man screamed.

"That's better. Now we're getting somewhere. What was her name?"

"I DON'T KNOW!" screamed the man, panicking that he was about to lose another finger.

"Okay, I'm not unreasonable. I understand you probably didn't know her name, but give me a description," Skelly said, ever so slightly moving the dagger that still pinned the man's hand to the fence, causing him to cry out in pain again.

Panting through the pain, he managed to say, "She was young … maybe sixteen … blonde hair … about my height. PLEASE! That's all I know … I need two hands to work … PLEASE!" he pleaded.

"That's good. But how am I to find someone in Helveel with only that information to go on? You need to give me something else to work with. Or I could simply remove another of your fingers to jog your memory," Skelly said coldly.

"NO! PLEASE! I ... I ... don't know anything else," the man begged.

"Okay, have it your way."

"NO WAIT! I remember something."

"Funny how pain jogs the memory isn't it," Skelly replied, grinning at Carter, who by this point was looking quite pale. "Go ahead, I'm listening."

"The girl ... after she sold me ... the horse ... she asked me ... which was the ... best thieves' guild ... here in Helveel ... I told..her ... to try the ... Ravens' guild—AARGH!"

Skelly removed the knife from the man's hand—and faster than anyone should be able to move—grabbed the back of the man's head, and placed it where his hand had been only a moment before. Holding a dagger to the man's eye, he said in a stone cold voice, "If you're lying to me, I'll come back and kill you—and it won't be fast. Do you understand?"

"YES!" the man screamed in absolute terror. Skelly let go of him and he collapsed into heap on the floor, clutching his mutilated hand to his chest, and crying like a child, as Skelly and Carter turned and calmly walked away.

It wasn't hard to find the headquarters of the Ravens' guild. It seemed almost everyone knew where it was located, and they soon arrived at the unassuming looking building. Two burly men stood guard outside the entrance, and as Skelly and Carter approached, they both removed weapons from their belts.

"Calm down lads. We're not here to cause you any trouble," Skelly reassured them, holding up his open hands to show he wasn't carrying any weapons.

"You've got no business here. Move along, before you get hurt," one of the guards said menacingly.

"I need to speak with whoever's in charge of

your recruiting here at the Ravens' guild," Skelly replied, not backing down.

"Well, he doesn't want to speak with you," the other man said laughing, as if what he had just said was the funniest thing he had ever come up with. Skelly wasn't amused, and the look in his eyes when he stared at the men, left them in no doubt either. Both men stopped laughing almost immediately, as the tension in the air rose rapidly; one false move, and everyone knew blood would be spilt.

Not looking half as confident as they had when Skelly and Carter had arrived, the first man said, "I can ask Tyray if he wants to speak with you, but he's going to ask what you want, and who you are?"

"What I want is none of your business. As for who I am, tell him I'm a fellow thief from Stelgad looking for a little professional courtesy," Skelly replied, with a forced smile that hid none of his contempt towards the two men.

One of the two men whispered something in the ear of the other, before saying, "Wait here. I'll ask him if he wants to see you." Then he opened the door and disappeared through it, closing it firmly behind him.

Several minutes passed before the door reopened, and the man who had taken the message reappeared, followed by eight other men. None of the men looked friendly, but Skelly had no doubt he could end them all without breaking a sweat if he had to. One of the men stepped forward, eyeing them both up and down, before saying, "My name is Tyray. I believe you wish to speak with me?"

"My name's Skelly. Thanks for taking the time to come and talk with me, I appreciate it."

"How can I help you Skelly?" Tyray asked calmly, as his men spread out all around him in a semi-circle, ready for any trouble that may arise.

"I'm looking for a girl …" Skelly started to say.

"Aren't we all?" Laughed one on the guards at the door.

Tyray turned sharply to look at the man, who visibly withered under his gaze, then he turned back to Skelly and said, "Sorry. Please continue. A girl?"

"Yes. A blonde girl, around sixteen years of age

and average height. I believe she approached you a few months ago to join your guild. She is wanted by our guild for the theft of guild property. Any information you have would be well appreciated." Skelly knew that every thieves' guild viewed the theft of its own property, by one of its own members, as the highest crime possible. Having an organization comprised solely of thieves, had to have the strictest possible consequences for anyone caught stealing from its own members. Usually it meant a death sentence without trial, and if this girl had gained employment here at the Ravens' guild, she would be ejected without question to face the accusing guild's justice. To do otherwise would risk a possible guild war, and the complete breakdown of thieves' justice within their organizations.

Skelly saw the glint of recognition in Tyray's eyes as he gave the description of the girl, but said nothing. He could see Tyray carefully working out the possibilities, and ramifications of the situation before responding.

"I have seen the girl you're describing. She

came here like you say a few months ago, but she was refused entry to the Ravens' guild. I knew nothing of her, and thought she might be a spy, sent by a rival guild. I'm sure you understand."

"Of course. Can you tell me where she is now?"

"What makes you think I would know where she is now?"

"Because, if you really thought she was a spy like you say, you would have had her followed for a while, to see if she reported back to another guild, and killed her if she had."

"And how do you know I would do that?"

"Because that's what I would have done," Skelly replied.

Tyray laughed, while nodding his head, "I see you're no '*wet behind the ears*' recruit Skelly. Yes, I did have her followed for over a week. Smart girl that one. She never approached another guild during that time. She was seen sleeping rough on the streets each night, and often visited the main gates each morning, like all the street kids do, to look for work. Last time she was seen, she was wearing a brown tunic and green trousers if that helps."

"Sir," one of the men addressed Tyray.

Tyray looked at him and bobbed his head for him to speak. "I have seen her a couple of times since we stopped following her. She was with a boy of about the same age last time I saw her." The man continued to give Skelly a description of the boy, and where he had seen them visiting.

"Thank you for your help. My guild appreciates your time and information, we would be happy to return the favour in the future if you ever find yourself in a similar situation. I also thank you for not requesting payment for the information, which of course, you were fully entitled to do. If, however, any of your guild spots this girl, I would be more than willing to pay for the information regarding her whereabouts. We will be staying at *The Golden Feather,* if she turns up."

"No need to pay. If she's spotted, I'll send word to you of her whereabouts. There's nothing I hate more in this world, than a thief who steals from their own. Just promise me one thing. Make sure she suffers before she dies," Tyray replied with conviction.

"Oh, you can count on that," replied Skelly with an evil grin.

Chapter Eight

Lusam woke up feeling happier than he could ever remember feeling in his whole life. The night before still fresh in his memory, of Neala's soft lips, and how wonderful they felt against his own. How they cuddled and caressed for hours, then talked into the small hours of the morning, about things he never thought he would share with anyone.

Today was both an end, and a new beginning for Lusam. Finally the books were almost all catalogued; today would be their last day before the work was complete. He was glad the tedious work was finally coming to an end, but he also knew he would miss this place too. This old underground monastery had given him so much, not least of which was the love of Neala, and the new magical knowledge he had gained, which he could use to create a new life for them both in the future. Feeling doubly blessed, he offered a prayer of thanks to Aysha, and asked that his good fortune may continue in the future they had both planned together the night before.

After getting dressed he headed to the book room for the final time, where he started moving the small remaining pile of books magically to be sorted alphabetically. He had only been there a few minutes, when Neala entered the room with a beaming smile on her face. She didn't offer him her usual morning greetings as she entered the room, but instead walked over to him, sat on his knee, and gave him a gentle kiss on his forehead, before saying, "Good morning my little mage."

Lusam smiled at the sound of her sultry voice, before kissing her lips, and saying in his best attempt to replicate the voice, "Good morning my little assassin." Neala playfully scowled and pouted at the description he used, but didn't comment on it any further. She then kissed his forehead once more and stood up.

"So, looks like our last day here then," she said, nodding towards the few books that were left in the small pile.

"Yeah, I was just thinking about that earlier. I think I'll miss this place you know. It's been good to us here. It's kept us warm and dry over winter, provided us with money and food, my new magic, and best of all, it gave me you." Neala beamed at his last comment.

"I'll miss it too, but at least I'll have you. I think we owe Mr Daffer more than he could ever know," Neala said.

Lusam laughed,"You're not kidding. How strange fate is. If I hadn't decided to go to the main gate that day, I'd never have met you, and none of this would ever have happened. Maybe we both would still be living on the streets, even now. Who knows?"

"I'm glad you did go to the gate."

"Me too," he agreed. "There aren't many books

left to do, maybe two hours at most. How about I come with you to get our supplies today?"

"That would be really nice," Neala said, offering her hand to hold. Lusam took her hand, and they left the book room and headed for the stairs to the shop. When they entered the shop, they both noticed Mr Daffer behind the counter slowly wrapping some books in brown paper.

"Good morning Mr Daffer," they both said almost in unison.

"Good morning," he replied glumly. Lusam thought it would be an ideal opportunity to inform Mr Daffer that this would be their last day, and thank him and Lucy for the chance of working for them both.

"Mr Daffer, I thought you would like to know all the books will be catalogued by the end of today. We would both like to thank you very much for giving us the opportunity to do the work for you," Lusam said, noticing Mr Daffer looked more than a little preoccupied.

"Oh, yes. Thank you both. That's good to hear," Mr Daffer replied, without any conviction in his voice at all.

"Would it be okay to thank Lucy too?" Neala asked hopefully.

Mr Daffer visibly sagged at the question. Lowering his head, he replied in a muffled voice, "I'm afraid not Neala. Lucy is gravely ill, and hasn't been awake since the day before yesterday. I will pass on your thanks if I am able." He could not hide the tears now falling freely from his eyes, as he looked away from Lusam and Neala.

Neala gasped at the bad news, before turning to Lusam, and with desperation in her voice said, "Lusam, you must help her! You can fix her with your mag … " Neala was cut short as Lusam squeezed her hand hard.

"Please can I speak with you alone for a minute," Lusam asked, nodding his head towards the basement door. Without waiting for a reply, he pulled Neala by the hand to the top of the stairs. Lusam looked back over his shoulder at Mr Daffer, but doubted he had even noticed their conversation he looked so grief-stricken. Opening the door, and

241

almost pulling Neala through after him, he turned back towards her. He was about to speak, when Neala angrily dragged her hand out of his grasp, and interrupted him.

"What's wrong with you Lusam? Lucy needs your help. Now! Have you forgotten what you said, not five minutes ago? We owe these people a huge amount. We certainly owe them enough to try and save one of their lives!" she almost screamed at him.

"I haven't forgotten anything! Neala believe me when I tell you, it's dangerous if we let people know about my magic."

"WHY? Why is it dangerous? Tell me." Lusam thought for a moment, then he realised he couldn't answer her question. He had been told over and over again by his grandmother when he was a child, that it was dangerous to let people know that he could wield magic, but she never told him why.

"I … I don't know," he replied deflated.

"You don't know! You're refusing to help, and you can't even tell me why! What happened to that person I met, the one who lived by his high and mighty moral code?" Neala was angrier than he ever thought possible, and he knew he didn't have a good enough reason to refuse to help Lucy. He also had no idea at all, if he could actually help her anyway. But there were two things he *did* know. The first was that these people deserved for him to at least try, and the second was, he certainly didn't want to lose Neala over something like this.

"Okay, I'll try. I'm not sure if I can do anything though, but I'll try my best. Whether it works or not, we must at least ask Mr Daffer to keep my secret safe," Lusam said quietly. Neala looked at Lusam, and nodded her head in agreement. She knew deep down that if he hadn't been genuinely concerned about keeping his secret safe, he would have agreed to help Lucy straight away, and if anything happened to Lusam because of this, she would never forgive herself.

"Okay, we'll make him promise never to reveal your secret, no matter what happens," Neala agreed.

Lusam instantly felt the tension leave the air between them. "Thanks Neala. I'm sorry I don't know why it's so important to keep my magic a secret, but I'm sure my grandmother had her reasons for making me promise never to reveal it. I'm sure if she had lived, she would have explained everything to me, and it would all make perfect sense. But unfortunately, I don't have all the answers," he said, in a soft calm voice.

"I understand your concerns, I really do, but we must help Lucy if we can. Come, let me talk with Mr Daffer. I'm sure he will agree to keep your secret safe." Neala took hold of Lusam's hand and led him back into the shop, towards the counter where Mr Daffer was still standing.

Neala noticed how lost in thought Mr Daffer was, as he absent-mindedly fiddled with the brown paper and string he was using to bind the books. "Excuse me Mr Daffer," she said, when he didn't seem to notice them both standing there. Mr Daffer turned his head towards them, but remained silent. Neala cleared her throat and tried to think of the best way to approach the subject with Mr Daffer, before deciding she should just say it.

"Mr Daffer, we have something important to tell you, but you must promise us you will never tell anyone else. Can you promise us this?"

Mr Daffer continued to stare blankly at her, as if he had not understood her words. "Please Mr Daffer. Lusam can help Lucy, but you must promise first." At the sound of Lucy's name, Mr Daffer seemed to become aware of his surroundings once more, and focused on the two of them standing there.

"The healers said nobody can help her now, child," Mr Daffer said in a defeated voice.

"Lusam may be able to help her, but I need you to promise you will keep his secret. Please Mr Daffer, promise me!" she said, pleading with him. Mr Daffer looked at her and nodded his head. It wasn't quite what Neala wanted, but she guessed it was all she would get out of Mr Daffer, so she continued, "Mr Daffer, Lusam can try to heal Lucy with his magic. He's really very good at it. Can you take us to her so he can try?"

Mr Daffer's face and mood changed so quickly it took Neala by surprise.

"Are you mad girl! Magic is not real! Please leave me alone. I have enough to worry about without your wild promises."

"But it's true! Just give him a chance and you'll see."

"GET OUT!" Mr Daffer shouted at them both, pointing towards the door.

Still holding Lusam's hand, she turned to him and said, "I'm sorry Lusam"

"Sorry for wha ... AARGH!"

Neala lifted Lusam's hand, and in the blink of an eye, cut the back of his hand with her dagger.

"What did you do that for?" he asked, holding his now bleeding hand in his other hand.

"Oh stop being a baby, it's only a scratch! Now you can show Mr Daffer you can use magic."

"I could have convinced him I had magic abilities by lifting one of his book cases or something, you didn't have to cut me!" he replied incredulously.

"Oh yeah, I never thought of that. Sorry," Neala said apologetically.

Mr Daffer stood there looking furious at the two

standing before him, one of whom, was now bleeding all over his clean floor. He was about to repeat his demand that they left his property immediately, when Lusam put his bleeding hand on top of the counter in front of Mr Daffer. Blood pooled onto the counter around Lusam's hand, as he began to focus on closing the wound.

Mr Daffer stood there with a look of complete shock and amazement, as the wound on Lusam's hand closed and vanished before his eyes. Once the wound was completely healed, Lusam wiped away the remaining blood to reveal a perfectly healed hand.

"How? How's that possible?" Mr Daffer whispered breathlessly, staring opened mouthed between Lusam's healed hand, and the two people standing before him.

"I told you, he can help Lucy with his magic, but you must promise never to reveal his secret to anyone. Ever," Neala repeated.

"Yes. Yes, I promise. I'll do anything if you help my Lucy. Please help her. Please!"

"I'll do my best to help her Mr Daffer, I

promise. But until I see her, I can't be certain I can cure her. You should know this before we start." Lusam didn't want to give Mr Daffer any false hope, just in case he couldn't help Lucy after all.

"Please! Anything you can do. I would be forever in your debt. Please follow me, I will take you to her right away." Mr Daffer almost ran out of the room, towards the dining room, where they had all shared a meal when they'd first arrived. Mr Daffer started to climb the wide curved staircase to the first floor, with Lusam and Neala following close behind. Lusam nudged Neala, and pointed up towards the incredible coloured glass dome, high up above their heads. It flooded the entire staircase with light containing all the colours of the rainbow.

"Wow!" she mouthed silently, almost falling up the stairs because she was unable to take her eyes off the beautiful glass dome.

When they reached the first landing, they were led down a long corridor to a room on the right. Mr Daffer knocked on the door softly, before opening the door slightly and peering inside. He then opened the door fully and gestured for them to enter. Lusam was shocked when he saw Lucy in the bed; she looked so pale as she slept. He noticed a woman standing next to her, administering a cool damp towel to her forehead. By the look of her clothes, Lusam guessed she must be a servant of some kind, and it alarmed him that someone else would be in the room when he performed his magic.

"How is she Lillian?" Mr Daffer asked in a quiet voice.

"She hasn't regained consciousness since yesterday, sir. I am afraid she may not last the night. Should I send for the healers again?"

"No. No thank you Lillian. Please, can you excuse us for a while. I will tend to Lucy for now."

"As you wish, sir," Lillian said, bowing slightly. She crossed the room, opened the door and exited onto the landing, before quietly closing the door behind her.

Mr Daffer waited a few seconds before speaking to Lusam. "I thought it would be better if we were alone when you did your … magic."

"Yes, thank you. I appreciate that," Lusam replied, very relieved he no longer had to worry about another person keeping his secret safe. He walked over to the side of the bed and sat down on the chair next to Lucy. He could not believe how nervous he was. It was as if the whole weight of the world was pressing down on him, and he had no idea if he could even help Lucy or not.

Neala could see the doubt and hesitation in Lusam's face as he sat there in front of Lucy. She walked over to him and held his hand.

She looked into his eyes and said, "I believe in you Lusam. I know you can do this. You'll do just fine." She smiled at him, then gave his hand a final squeeze, before stepping back and allowing him to do whatever he needed to do. Lusam bobbed his head towards her, then turned to face Lucy. He searched his newly found knowledge for a way to begin, but soon realised it was obvious he must first find out what was actually wrong with Lucy. Focusing hard, he sent out his mage-sight to search inside Lucy's body for the cause of her illness. It took only a few minutes to find the problem. Lucy had some kind of growth in her body. It appeared to be eating away at the surrounding body tissue, and was also stopping her vital organs functioning properly. He also noticed the growth was slowly poisoning her blood. He knew he couldn't just break up the object, as that would surely kill her from the poisoning of her blood. It needed to be removed, but it was so deep inside her he had no idea how to do it.

Lusam retracted his mage-sight from within Lucy's body, and sat back heavily in the chair.

"What's up? What did you find? Can you heal her?" asked Mr Daffer desperately.

"I found something inside her, and it needs to be removed. But, I'm unsure how to do it without killing her."

"There must be something you can do? Please. Please try." Mr Daffer moved to the other side of the bed and took hold of Lucy's other hand, while tears flowed freely down his cheeks and dripped onto the pristine white sheets. Lusam racked his brain for a solution, but all he could come up with was a crazy idea that he doubted would work due to its complexity. The only thing he could think of doing, was to create an opening in Lucy's skin and remove the growth that way. The problem was, the growth would have to be pulverized into minute pieces, so it was able to pass through the small blood vessels and routes necessary to reach the outside world. He couldn't allow the poison to enter her bloodstream, or it would kill her for sure.

He would again have to use his force-field magic, but this time, on a minuscule level. He needed to contain the broken up growth, and then manoeuvre it to an incision made in Lucy's skin, all the time, keeping track of thousands, if not tens of thousands of tiny fragments. If a single fragment was left inside her, he felt sure it could grow again and claim her life in the future. Thinking back to the days spent on the side of the river collecting gold, he knew his limitations in the number of object he could track and manipulate at any given time, and he also knew this would be many times that number.

Lusam explained in detail what he had seen to

the others, and then told them of his plan to remove it, and why it was not possible, due to the incredible number of particles that would need to be dealt with and manipulated simultaneously. Mr Daffer sat there holding his wife's hand, and cried in silence.

"There must be a way to do it. There has to be," Neala said out loud to herself. She sat there for several minutes, thinking in a room so quiet, she could hear her own heartbeat. "Is it possible to remove a small part at a time?" she asked Lusam hopefully. "Then you wouldn't have to deal with as many parts all at once."

Lusam took a loud intake of breath. It almost sounded as if he had been holding his breath since finishing his explanation. "I suppose it's possible, but I think it would take an awful long time to achieve."

Thinking about the problem in more detail, he realised he could contain the growth in a force-field, then take a small portion at a time into a second force-field to remove from her body. He would also have to maintain a third force-field at the skin surface, to stop her bleeding to death while the procedure took place. He felt dizzy at the complexity of it all, and he also had no idea how long it would take to do. Could he even maintain his magic that long non-stop? He didn't know. If his magic failed, the poison would enter Lucy's bloodstream and kill her for sure.

He took a long steadying breath, then began to explain the concept of what he would have to do if he attempted the procedure. When he finished speaking, he was met with a wall of silence. It was obvious that both Mr Daffer and Neala understood the enormity of such an undertaking, and the potential risks involved to Lucy.

Mr Daffer stood up from his chair, bent over and kissed Lucy tenderly on her forehead. "I Love you Lucy," he whispered in her ear. Then he walked slowly around the foot of the bed, and came to stand before Lusam. He placed a hand on Lusam's shoulder, took a deep steadying breath, and spoke what must have been the hardest words of his life, "Although I could never fully understand what you must do to try and save Lucy, I do understand how incredibly difficult it must be for you. But, even knowing that

Lucy may die should it not work, I would still ask that you at least try to save her. Please know that I will not place blame upon you Lusam, should your efforts be in vain, and neither should you blame yourself if such comes to pass."

Lusam could feel Mr Daffer's hand tremble on his shoulder. He sensed the incredible self control of the man, being able to stand there and request that he still try to save Lucy, even knowing if he should fail, the love of his life would surely die. Lusam placed his hand on top of Mr Daffer's, and looking him directly in the eyes, he replied,

"I will give it all I have, I promise. You've both given us so much, and it's now time we tried to repay you for your kindness." Lusam's words were too much for Mr Daffer, he squeezed Lusam's shoulder one more time, then turned his head away, as a flurry of tears rolled down his face. Neala stepped forward to steady him, and helped him back to his chair next to his unconscious wife.

Lusam looked over at Neala, and she nodded at his unspoken question of whether he should begin.

With a deep breath, and a prayer to Aysha to grant him the strength to complete his task, he closed his eyes, and sent forth his mage-sight to once again locate the growth within Lucy's body.

Finding the growth, he surrounded it with a force-field, and carefully detached it from its blood supply and surrounding tissue. Carefully, he repaired the area and then made sure there was no further internal bleeding, before beginning the long process of removing the mass. Taking a small piece of the growth and separating it off from the main mass into a second force-field, he began to manoeuvre the tiny object through Lucy's vascular system, and towards the surface of her skin. He had no idea there were so many blood vessels inside a human body; it was like the largest and most complex maze he could have ever have imagined.

Finally, he found a route to the surface of Lucy's skin towards her lower abdomen. Parting her skin with his magic, and placing yet another force-field over the cut to stop the bleeding, he let the small piece of growth pass through the opening, and removed it from Lucy's body. Not able to break his concentration and look for himself, he just hoped that Neala was there to clean away the parts of the growth he was removing from Lucy's body as they emerged.

Countless hours went by, and still Lusam had not removed all of the growth. Neala had no idea how he was able to maintain his concentration for so long without even moving. If it wasn't for the small glistening specks of material appearing every few minutes on the surface of Lucy's skin, and the beads of sweat on Lusam's forehead—which seemed to becoming more noticeable by the minute—she would have assumed Lusam had fallen asleep, sitting upright in his chair.

Lusam was almost completely exhausted. He could sense his magic reserves were almost depleted. All he could think about, was a lesson he had been taught by his grandmother so long ago about the overuse of magic. She had told him: *"Never attempt to use too much magic at once, for if the magic reserve of any mage becomes empty, it would surely kill them.*" He knew that point wasn't far off, and would certainly come before he had finished his task.

His head pounded with the effort, and his heart raced at the thought of the consequences of failure. Lucy would surely die. Mr Daffer would be devastated at the loss of his wife, but most of all, he feared letting Neala down, by not being able to keep his promise of a life together. Without Lusam's magic, Neala would be once again forced to live on the streets. No! He could not let that happen! He would not let that happen! Desperately, he searched for an answer. All he needed was a little more magic, his task was almost complete, but he was almost out of time.

Lusam knew the magic within him would be replaced over time, like a leaking roof would eventually fill a bowl left to catch the rain. Everybody and everything had magic within it, and surrounding it. This was a lesson he had learned many years ago, but until this moment, it had not really meant that much to him. He needed to get some of that magic, and fast. Before his own was completely used up, and both he and Lucy died in the process.

"That's it! Lucy!" he thought to himself. Lucy was not a magic-user, he knew that from her aura, but she would have a certain amount of magic within her, like all living beings. He just hoped it would be enough to complete his task. The trick would be, not to take it all, and end up killing her that way instead.

He had absolutely no idea how he could use Lucy's store of magic, or even if it was possible to do so. Running out of time, he once again prayed for guidance, before attempting to siphon off some of Lucy's magic into his own store. There seemed to be some kind of natural barrier containing the magic within Lucy, and it took him several minutes to find a way to penetrate the barrier. Once he eventually found a way to get through her barrier, he found it very easy to take her magic into his own reserve. It felt like a cool drink of water quenching his thirst after a long desert crossing. It was only a small amount of magic compared to what he was able to hold, but maybe it would be enough. Working as fast as he dared, he guided the last of the growth to the surface of Lucy's skin, before checking one final time it had all been removed. He removed the force-field inside Lucy's body that had held the growth, and then repaired the cut to her skin. With only seconds to spare, he opened his eyes and allowed himself a small smile. The room spun in front of his eyes, and his vision faded to black, as he felt himself falling. The last thing he heard was Neala calling his name, before the darkness claimed him.

Chapter Nine

Renn watched the agent of Aamon from the shadows, as he had done now for so long. He had been tempted many times to end the life of this necromancer, none more so, than when he had raised the dead body in that back alley with his dark magic, and sent it out into the city to do his evil bidding. The death and destruction it would have caused if Renn had not been there to deal with it, made him even more inclined to end the life of this evil man. Taking a deep breath, he steadied his overwhelming desire to kill him, and reminded himself of why he was here. Why he had spent over a year following this man in the shadows, sleeping rough on the streets and in alleyways, waiting and hoping, that one day he would lead him to the boy-mage known as Lusam, who held so much promise for the land of Afaraon.

Today, as he watched the agent of Aamon, he noticed some strange behaviour he hadn't seen before. He seemed to be walking several paces, then stopping, closing his eyes, using some sort magic spell, then walking again. He repeated this process for several hours, seemingly not concerned at all if anyone saw him or not. Each time he stopped, Renn could see his aura flash brighter with the use of magic. He seemed to be listening to something in the distance, and each time he stopped and closed his eyes, his head would flick slightly from side to side, as if he were trying to catch a distant voice on the breeze.

All morning, and into the early afternoon, the agent of Aamon had been slowly making his way towards the east district of the city. Many people passing by had given him strange looks, and a few of the less savoury types had even thrown verbal abuse at him, but he never once seemed to notice any of them. Renn was sure he could have come out of the shadows in plain sight and followed two footsteps behind him, and still not have been seen. It was obvious he had sensed something that Renn could not.

Renn could sense magic in others, but he was no mage. He was a paladin of Aysha, and he gained his power through his devotion to his God. Paladins often wielded weapons of power and sometimes shields, both contained blessings from their God, and the strength of those weapons were directly linked to the strength of their faith. Renn wielded both sword and shield, his devotion and faith were unquestionable.

It was late afternoon when the agent of Aamon suddenly stopped his strange behaviour. He was standing in the middle of the market square with his eyes closed, when to anyone that happened to be looking at him, he seemed to simply wake up from a deep sleep. His eyes snapped open and he looked about at his surroundings, as if he had no idea where he was. He looked up at the sun, as if to judge the time of day, then took another quick look around him, before heading straight for an inn on the opposite side of the market square. Renn guessed whatever he was listening to had stopped, but couldn't be sure. As luck would have it, another inn shared the market square directly opposite the first. Normally, Renn would have to sleep outside whichever inn the agent of Aamon chose to stay at, but today luck was on his side, and he could find warmth, comfort, and a meal inside the inn opposite, while he watched and waited for his quarry to reappear.

Renn entered the inn via the main entrance facing the market square. His eyes quickly adjusting to the dimly lit interior. The room was larger than he would have guessed from outside. It held maybe a dozen large round tables with stools and benches; which provided seating for the many patrons who currently occupied them. A large fire was set in the hearth at the far end of the room, giving off a pleasant smell of pine from the burning wood. Renn instinctively scanned the room for potential threats, but found none. Most looked like they were traders conducting friendly business over a lunchtime ale or two. The low down rumble of quiet conversation quickly fell silent, as one after another of the patrons noticed the strange man now standing in the room.

Renn knew how threatening he must look standing there in his filthy clothes, with a large shield strapped to his back and a sword at his waist. He nodded a greeting to the men sitting at the closest table, attempting to lessen the now palpable tension filling the air. If he'd not been on his secret mission to follow the agent of Aamon, he would have worn his sigil of Aysha in plain view around his neck. The sigil was instantly recognizable by anyone in the land of Afaraon, and would have clearly marked him as a paladin of Aysha. Paladins were held in extremely high regard throughout the land, as defenders of Afaraon and its people.

He had no doubt his reception here would have been completely different if he had been wearing his sigil in plain sight. However, he could not risk it becoming common knowledge around Helveel, that a paladin of Aysha was within its walls. If the agent of

Aamon heard rumours that a paladin might be here in Helveel, all may be lost, and the last year spent following him would have been for nothing.

Renn slowly approached the counter. The barkeep had already stopped what he was doing, watching nervously as Renn approached. The barkeep cleared his throat and took a step back, placing a freshly dried flagon on the shelf at the back of the bar. Renn knew he was only trying to put himself out of the reach of his sword, just in case he *was* as dangerous as he looked.

"Can I help you?" the barkeep asked, in a calm even tone. Renn was impressed at his ability to hold his nerve, but felt guilty at causing him discomfort.

"I'd like a room please. South facing with a window and a bathtub. A hot meal in my room, and most importantly, some privacy."

"I'm sorry, we're fully booked at the moment, sir. Maybe the Royal Inn across the street can accommodate you," the barkeep said nervously.

Renn stared at the man. With each heartbeat the barkeep withered under his gaze. Without breaking eye contact Renn removed his coin pouch, produced a gold coin, and placed it on the counter in front of him. The Barkeep momentarily let his eyes flick to the coin, and Renn could see them instantly light up at the sight of gold. Renn added a second gold coin to the first, then slowly pushed the two gold coins forward on the counter.

"I'm sure you can find a room for me here at your inn. It looks a much better establishment than the Royal Inn across the square," Renn replied, smiling at the barkeep's new predicament. Did he let this potentially dangerous man stay here and take the two gold coins, or still refuse him, and throw away a weeks worth of money to his competitor across the street?

Renn knew all about human nature, and so knew the answer even before the barkeep spoke a word. "Actually, I think we do have a south facing room available tonight sir, now that I think about it," he said, licking his lips subconsciously, eyes darting between Renn and the coins laid out between them. Renn smiled at the man, pushing the coins to the rear of the counter, then taking a step back to give the man some room.

"Excellent. Thank you," replied Renn.

For a large man he moved fast to scoop up the gold coins from the counter, then went to the key-hook at the rear of the bar area; always staying out of range of any danger. He lifted a room key from one of the many hooks, then offered it at arms length to Renn across the bar.

"Room seven, on the second floor. I will have the bathtub and food brought to your room shortly. Will that be all sir?" he asked.

"Yes. Thank you for your hospitality," Renn replied, still smiling at the man standing as far away from him as was possible. He took the key and headed for the stairs to his room. He could feel every eye in the room follow him as he started to climb the staircase. As he turned the corner, out of sight, he paused, and heard the conversations restart again, as if he'd never been there. He chuckled to himself. Renn knew, that given a choice of speculating as to why a heavily armed man had just entered the establishment, or talking about business opportunities and making money, that they would choose the latter and he would be very soon forgotten.

He stopped outside the door marked number seven. It was a heavy dark wooden door, with a good quality lock and heavy hinges. *People who stayed here obviously viewed security as a priority*, Renn thought. He guessed many traders would frequent these rooms on their way to and from their business dealings, and if they were carrying large sums of coins, they would certainly want well-made doors and locks.

Renn unlocked the door and entered the room. He quickly walked over to the large window, and was relieved to see it offered a fantastic view of not only the inn opposite, but the whole of the market square below. The room offered only basic comforts, but it was clean and well maintained. There was a single wardrobe, two wooden dining chairs and a small table. The bed was a large four post bed with a small cabinet at each side, and an oil filled lamp on each. He looked at the large comfortable looking bed with regret, knowing he would be spending the night in a chair by the window, keeping watch, instead of sampling its warmth and comfort.

Renn offered a prayer to Aysha for providing him with his new creature comforts, and the first opportunity in a long time to take a warm bath. He picked up one of the chairs and moved it to the window, then did the same with the small square-top table. He then removed his shield and placed it at the bottom of the bed, and was halfway through unbuckling his sword, when a knock came at the door.

"Enter," Renn said, loud enough for them to hear at the other side of the door.

In walked a young boy of about twelve-years-old, carrying a tray of food and drink. He noticed Renn's hand near his sword, and froze to the spot with a look of sheer terror on his face. Renn saw the boy's reaction, and nodded his head towards the table. "Please put it on the table over by the window," Renn said, removing his sword belt and tossing it onto the bed. The boy's eyes followed the sword until it hit the bed, then after several seconds staring at it, he seemed to remember Renn had just spoken to him.

"Oh … yes sir. Sorry, of course," he stammered, while walking to the table near the window and depositing his tray of food. "Would there be anything else sir?" he asked, backing towards the door, as if he had been trapped in a room with a rabid wolf. Renn couldn't help but laugh at the boy's nervousness. He removed a silver coin from his pouch and tossed it through the air towards the boy. The boy caught it deftly in mid-air, and his nervousness was instantly replaced with a look of complete joy at receiving a silver coin.

"Nothing else for right now, thanks. I'd like my bathtub and water in about an hour, if you'd be kind enough to inform the barkeep on your way back."

"Sure thing, sir. Enjoy your food," he replied, looking a lot happier than when he first arrived.

Renn watched the boy leave and close the door gently behind himself, before returning to the window seat to enjoy his food. It was the first hot meal he'd had for many a month, and the smell alone almost made him dizzy. Secretly, he hoped the agent of Aamon would stay at the inn opposite for at least a few days, but the way he had seen him act today, he doubted that would be the case. Something had obviously got his attention, and Renn couldn't see him wanting to lose the scent of whatever he'd been following for most of that day; only time would tell. Renn let out a small sigh, and lost himself in the simple pleasure of his hot food.

It seemed like only a few minutes since he had finished his food, before another knock brought his attention back to the door again.

"Enter," he said loudly. The door opened, and the same boy brought in a tin bathtub and placed it down in front of the fire. He was followed by three younger boys, all carrying buckets of steaming hot water. The younger boys entered the room, all three of them immediately looking towards the bed, where Renn's sword still lay. The older boy had probably been telling tales to the younger ones, and now they had all seen his *"fabled sword,"* it must mean the rest of his story was also true, whatever that story was.

The three younger boys stood staring open-mouthed at Renn's shield and sword lying on the bed, until the older boy clattered the tin bathtub onto the floor it in front of the fireplace, instantly bringing all three of them back to reality with a start. All three visibly jumped at the sudden sound, one even spilling part of the contents of his bucket down himself. Each boy quickly emptied their hot water into the bathtub, then turned to leave the room, none of them daring to look back towards Renn as they left. The older boy stepped back away from the bathtub towards the door behind him, before asking, "Is there anything else you require, sir."

"No, that will be all thank you. Oh … you can tell me one thing though."

Looking a little worried, the boy replied, "What's that sir?"

Smiling at the boy, Renn asked, "Was it a good story you told your small friends?" The boy couldn't help himself as a huge grin spread across his face.

"Aye. That it was, sir," he replied, as he backed out of the room struggling to contain his own amusement. When the door closed Renn couldn't help chuckling to himself either, as he imagined the outrageous stories that must now be spreading like wildfire among the younger employees of the inn.

Removing a small mirror from his pouch, he placed it on the window sill, so it would give him a clear view of the entrance to the inn opposite, while he took his bath. Then he undressed and stepped into the first warm bath he'd had in far too many months. As he sank down into the steaming hot water, he thanked Aysha once again for allowing him these small luxuries, but knew before long, that his work would recommence in the pursuit of the necromancer; hopefully leading him to the boy-mage known as Lusam.

Chapter Ten

Lusam stirred to the noise of the curtains being drawn back. The light flooded into the room, and a headache, the likes of which he had never known in his life, erupted behind his closed eyelids. He groaned and tried to lift the blankets higher to shield his eyes, but the effort of moving his arms only intensified the pain in his head. The room was far too bright to open his eyes, but he did hear someone pass by the bottom of his bed and leave through the door, before quietly closing it behind them.

Slowly his eyes adjusted to the bright light of the room, and he tentatively opened his eyes to see where he was. The last thing he remembered was trying to heal Lucy, but he couldn't remember if he had succeeded or not. In fact, he couldn't remember much of anything from that day. He tried to sit up in the bed, but again, the slight effort of moving brought on the intense pain in his head once more. Bright spots danced across his vision, and a fresh wave of nausea threatened to overtake him. Lying back and panting through the pain, he managed to steady himself, before attempting to open his eyes again. Deciding against trying to move again, he glanced around the room to take in his surroundings. Realisation hit him like a bolt of lightning: he was in Lucy's bed. That must mean he'd failed in his attempt to save her.

Lusam's heart sank at the thought of what Mr Daffer must be going through right now. He doubted he could ever look him in the eyes again without feeling guilty for what he had done. He felt devastated beyond words, and wondered if even Neala could ever forgive him. Unable to face the possibility of losing Neala, he closed his eyes, and tried to shut out the cruel world outside.

He could hear running footsteps coming from the hallway outside the bedroom door, then the door flew open, banging loudly against the wardrobe standing just to the side of it. Lusam was sure Mr Daffer had come to exact his revenge over losing his wife to his failed magic. He couldn't blame him either. He decided at that moment not to resist whatever he did to him. Not that he was in any shape to do so, anyway.

"LUSAM! YOU'RE AWAKE!" shouted a familiar voice. Lusam's head throbbed with every word, but hearing that voice was worth any amount of pain.

"Neala," he croaked back. Even his voice wouldn't obey his commands; he sounded like he had eaten a bucket full of sand. Before he could even fully open his eyes, Neala had him held tight in her embrace, and was kissing him all over his very tender head. He opened his eyes to find her face very close to his own, with tears rolling down her cheeks.

"I'm sorry Neala. I tried. I really did. I'm so sorry," he croaked. Neala smiled at him, shook her head slightly, then kissed him on his forehead, before standing up and moving away from his bedside. Standing there behind her, was the best sight Lusam could ever have wished to see. "Lucy! You're alive … "

"Yes, thanks to you I am," she replied. Mr Daffer suddenly appeared in the doorway behind her, and came to stand by her side. He reached down to take hold of Lucy's hand and squeezed it tightly, before turning back to Lusam.

"We can never thank you enough for what you have done for us Lusam. If there is anything you ever need, and it's within our power to grant it, you need only ask."

"That's very kind of you Mr Daffer, but seeing Lucy well is reward enough. You've both done so much for us already. I'm just glad we were able to repay some of your kindness," Lusam replied, then after a moments hesitation he added, "although, if it's not too much trouble, maybe some food and a drink would be great. I'm starving!"

"Oh … now I know he's going to be fine,"

Neala said, rolling her eyes at him. Lusam just smiled at her, while the rest of them laughed at Neala's comments.

After eating what tasted like the best food of his life, and drinking enough water to fill half a bathtub, he found himself with enough energy to get out of bed and search out his clothes. His head still hurt, but nothing like it had when he first awoke. He managed to get dressed and sit himself in the chair next to the window. The window overlooked the alley behind the shop, and it immediately reminded Lusam of the alley behind the baker's shop, where he'd spent so many days and nights. How different his life was now. How much easier it would be from now on. How much happier he would be now he had Neala. He knew he loved her, and he knew she loved him. Surely their future together would be great.

His day-dreaming was interrupted by a knock at the door, followed by the click of the door opening. Neala's smiling face appeared from behind the door.

"Ah, good, you're awake," she said, as she

entered the room and closed the door gently behind her. She walked over to where Lusam was sat looking out of the window, and stood behind him with her hands on his shoulders. Bending down, she kissed the top of his head, before whispering in his ear, "I thought I'd lost you forever. Please, don't ever do that to me again. I was so worried about you."

"How long was I unconscious?" he asked, reaching up to hold one of her hands.

"Over four days."

"FOUR DAYS?" Lusam screeched, spinning around to face her, and immediately wishing he hadn't, as his head swam in pain again from the sudden movement. Holding his head in both hands, he repeated his question much more sedately, "Four days? I was asleep for four days?"

"Almost five, actually. I was so worried about you Lusam. I would never have forgiven myself if you hadn't come back to me. It was my fault I forced you into trying to heal Lucy, it could have cost you your life. I'm so sorry."

"It didn't. And you were right to make me try.

280

Lucy is healthy again, and apart from this insane headache, I'm fine too. In a day or two I'm sure I'll be back to full strength again. Then we can finish the last of the books, and celebrate a job well done," he said, smiling at her.

"Don't worry about the books. I've already finished cataloguing them while you were unconscious. I was at my wits' end with worry, and I had to keep my mind occupied, or I would have gone insane."

"Wow! ... Really? I'm so proud of you Neala. Well done!" he said, beaming with pride.

"It was easy. I had a great teacher," she replied, ginning from ear to ear.

Lusam laughed at her compliment and teased her with, "Yes, I guess you did."

Rolling her eyes at his statement, but not biting at the bait, she asked, "If you feel well enough by the day after tomorrow, there's a carnival in town. Maybe you could take me there to celebrate our success?"

"That sounds like a great idea. I'm sure I'll be fine by then. I feel almost back to full strength already," he said, standing up to give her a passionate kiss.

After a few moments she freed herself from his kiss, pushed him away slightly, then replied grinning, "Yes, I can tell you're feeling better." Then Neala turned and headed for the door. When she reached the door, she opened it, then turned back towards Lusam. "Save your strength. You never know, you might need it later," she said, winking at him, as the door closed behind her. *Now I know for certain I won't get any more sleep today,* Lusam thought to himself.

Lusam was lying on his bed, when a quiet knock at his door startled him. "Come in," he said, loud enough for whoever was outside the door to hear. The door opened and a woman peered around the door into his room. He recognised her as the maid who had been attending Lucy when he first came to this room. "Lillian isn't it?" Lusam asked.

"Yes sir, that's correct. Sorry to intrude, but I'm here to inform you that the evening meal will be served shortly. If you feel well enough, you're welcome to join the others in the dining room, in around fifteen minutes."

"Thank you Lillian. I'll be down shortly."

"Very good, sir," Lillian replied, but hesitated in leaving the room. Instead, she stood there silently, looking a little apprehensive.

"May I help you with something else Lillian?"

"I … I would like to thank you for whatever you did to help Mrs Daffer. I have no idea how you did what you did, but thank you."

Not knowing just how much she *did* know, Lusam simply smiled and replied, "You're welcome. I'm glad I could help." Lillian nodded, smiled back and left the room.

Ten minutes later, Lusam entered the dining room to find Mr Daffer, Lucy and Neala already seated at the table. "Ah, glad you felt up to joining us Lusam. Please, take a seat. Dinner will be served shortly," Mr Daffer announced.

"Thank you," Lusam replied, taking a seat next to Neala. "How are you feeling Lucy?"

"I feel almost as good as new, thanks to you

Lusam. How about you? You still look a little tired to me."

"Oh, I'm fine now thanks Lucy. Nothing a good night's sleep won't fix, I'm sure."

"Well, you are both welcome to stay here as long as you like with us. Please don't think you have to leave now that your work is finished. We owe you a debt that could never be repaid, so as far as we are concerned, you're as good as family from now on," said Mr Daffer.

Lusam didn't really know how to react to what Mr Daffer had just said, so he looked to Neala, who obviously had been told the same news already; because she didn't look half as shocked as she should have been.

"Er … wow! Thanks Mr and Mrs Daffer. I don't know what to say, except, thank you."

"You're more than welcome Lusam," Lucy replied, obviously amused by the surprise showing on his face. Just as Lusam was desperately trying to think of something to say—to fill the awkward silence—Lillian emerged through the double doors with the first dishes of the evening meal.

"Ah … wonderful, dinner has arrived," announced Mr Daffer, breaking the silence.

"Is everything alright Lusam?" asked Lucy, looking a little concerned at how quiet he had become since he'd been given the news.

"Yes … yes of course. Why shouldn't it be?" replied Lusam, squirming a little in his seat as he said it.

"It's just you seem a little … preoccupied ever since we told you that you were both welcome to stay here as long as you like with us. I thought you might be happy here," Lucy said, catching him completely off guard.

"Oh, no. I mean yes. Yes of course we'd be happy here with you both. Your offer is a very kind one. I … we … Neala and me, kind of had plans for after we finished here, but we haven't had time to talk since before, you know, before what just happened," Lusam stammered, his face flushing to a bright red.

"Oh, is that all it is?" asked Lucy, looking relieved. "I thought we had done something to offend you in some way."

"No … no, not at all," Lusam quickly replied. "You've both been incredibly kind to us. The last thing I want to do is insult either of you by refusing your generous offer, especially after all you have done for us."

He was about to continue, when Lucy laughed and said, "Oh, I'm sorry Lusam. I think you may have misunderstood our intentions. Of course you'll have plans for your future together, you're both very young still. You should know the offer remains open for you both, no matter what you decide to do now. If you decide to go off together and explore the world now, but need somewhere to stay in the future, our home will always be open to you both. What we're really trying to say is: if you ever need help, now, or in the future, and it's within our power to help, we would always do so willingly, you need only ask."

Lusam sat at the table trying to absorb the information that Lucy had just given him. He now had a home to return to, and for the first time in a long time, he also had a place he could call home.

He was lost deep in thought when Neala took hold of his hand and gave it a small squeeze, bringing him back to the present. "I don't really know how to thank you both for your kindness," Lusam replied, slightly choked up and with tears of joy starting to form in his eyes.

"Nonsense! We have thanks enough already. I have my Lucy back, when I thought I had lost her forever. So I propose a toast … To the future, and whatever it brings!" said Mr Daffer, raising his glass. They all lifted their glasses and repeated the toast; *'To the future, and whatever it brings.'*

It was the day of the carnival, and both Neala and Lusam were looking forward to spending some time together, as well as spending some of their hard-earned cash. Lusam had never been to a carnival before. Once a year the carnival would come to Helveel, but the street kids were forbidden to enter the town square while it was running. Any street kid caught within the town square while the carnival was taking place, would be treated as a thief and dealt with accordingly. Once the carnival had packed up and left the town square, it became rich pickings for the street kids. So much wasted food and other items lay discarded all around the square, the guards turned a blind eye to the street kids taking their fill. Lusam knew the more the kids cleaned away, the less the local officials would need to arrange to be removed later.

Lusam never tried his luck with any of the items left behind by the carnival. The amount and relative quality of the plunder meant it was often fought over by the street kids. They would form gangs and alliances days before the carnival would even arrive. It was a dangerous time of year to be a lone street kid: many found themselves targets of the gangs around that time. As fast as the gangs and alliances were formed, they would just as quickly disappear again, as soon as the carnival had left town and it's remains fully plundered.

Lusam remembered his first year in Helveel, when he almost became a victim of one of these gangs, but he'd been fortunate enough to lose them in the back streets of Helveel. He remained mostly in his grate for the next few days until the carnival had left town, and things returned to normality again. The following year he had decided not to take any chances, and instead spent the time in the forest outside Helveel.

This year would be different. He was no longer a street kid of Helveel. He would have money in his pocket to spend and clean clothes on his back. No one could accuse him or Neala of being street kids any longer, they would be free citizens of Helveel, and would have the freedom of the city at last.

Mr Daffer had paid them for their work cataloguing the books, and together with the gold coins Lusam had made from the river, they each now had a good sum of money. Lusam had never had more than a coin or two in his pocket in his whole life. He didn't really know how to deal with having such a large amount of money on his person at any one time.

Neala had shown him how, and where, best to carry his coins for safety, using the special leather coin pouches they'd bought in Helveel. She'd also suggested that they leave most of their coins in one of the chests, in the basement of the shop, while they visited the carnival, and only take with them what they might need for that day.

Mr Daffer had offered them both rooms upstairs in the main house after Lusam had recovered, but both Lusam and Neala felt more relaxed in their old sleeping cells, and had politely refused his offer. Lusam looked around his sleeping cell and knew he would really miss this place when they finally left. He was very happy knowing he could return here if he needed to, or wanted to, in the future for any reason.

"Hey! Are you ignoring me?" Neala asked.

"Er … no. Why?" Lusam replied confused, standing up from his bed.

"I called your name three times. I thought you'd gone without me."

"Sorry … I was just thinking about things, that's all. Are you ready to go?"

"That's what I was trying to ask you. So, I guess we're ready then."

"Great. How much money do you think we should take with us?" Lusam asked, weighing his coin pouch in his hand.

"I doubt we'll need more than one gold between us. But make sure you take small value coins, and distribute them in different pockets. I know the street kids are not permitted to be there, but there'll certainly be plenty of cutpurses and pickpockets watching the crowds. You don't want to be pulling out large numbers of coins, or high value coins, in plain view," Neala said, in a mother to child type voice.

"Okay, thanks. I'll do that," Lusam replied sheepishly.

"Good, let's go then. Oh … wait a minute. I'll be right back," Neala said, as she quickly vanished from Lusam's room and headed for her own sleeping cell. One minute later she reappeared in Lusam's doorway, still buckling on her throwing knife belt.

"We're going to the carnival, what do you need those for? Unless you intend to entertain the crowd with a knife throwing exhibition," he said, with a smug look on his face.

"Ha! Ha! Very funny! You never know when you might need your weapons. It's always better to have them with you, than find out later that you need them, and not have them."

"I suppose so," agreed Lusam; less than convinced. Clicking his fingers together in a flamboyant gesture, he extinguished the light that was glowing on the ceiling of his cell, plunging it into darkness as he left the room and headed for the stairs to the shop above. Neala just rolled her eyes and followed in his wake, muttering something about boys and show-offs to herself. Lusam just smiled to himself, and pretended not to hear her.

As they approached the carnival they could hear the music playing in the distance, and smell the deliciously tempting foods on offer at the numerous stalls around the town square. People filled the whole area, all buffeting each other for a better view of the latest act on stage at the far end of the square. Jugglers dressed in motley costumes dotted the crowd, some high up on stilts, others balancing on the shoulders of their partners. One was juggling with a set of flaming torches, while another used vicious looking knifes. Everywhere they looked, something was happening.

There were signs depicting various acts and attractions. Each sign had both a picture representing the activity, and the words above it for the few people who could read.

"What should we see first?" Lusam asked, still overawed by the sheer scale of the event.

"I'm not sure. Maybe we should just work our way around and see what we find as we go?" Neala suggested.

"Sounds like a good enough plan to me," Lusam agreed, taking hold of Neala's hand as they started making their way towards the first tent. Outside, there was a large picture board depicting a knife and a lady wearing a tunic and leggings. Above the picture were the words: *The Great Ormando*.

"I wonder what this is?" Lusam asked. A skinny man wearing a black suit overheard his question, and answered before Neala even had the chance.

"Only one silver coin each to witness something so spectacular, you will be telling your grandchildren about it years from now. Roll up! Roll up! The show is about to start. Don't miss this opportunity to witness the amazing skill of the Great Ormando!"

"What do you think? Shall we go see? Come on, let's go see this amazing Great Ormando," Lusam said excitedly, all the time tugging on Neala's hand.

"Okay, okay, let's go see what all the fuss is about," Neala agreed.

Lusam placed two silver coins in the palm of the skinny man's hand, and then headed directly for the door to the large tent, with Neala following close behind him. When they entered the tent they saw several rows of chairs, most of which were empty, and a large stage at the front. Lusam headed directly for a seat on the front row, and Neala followed his example. They sat down, still holding hands, while Lusam looked around the large tent with a child's curiosity.

Neala smiled at his reaction to a simple tent

containing nothing more than a few props of a carnival attraction. It was then she actually realised just how restricted Lusam's childhood and adolescent years must have been. Although she'd not had a family in the usual sense of the word, she had grown up with a lot of freedom. She had seen many carnivals over the years, even working as a thief at some. To her, this was normal. To Lusam it was something special. She loved his innocence, and she loved *him* beyond words. She released his hand and turned his face towards her. Looking into his innocent eyes she whispered, "I love you Lusam."

Lusam flushed a little at her unexpected declaration, but returned the words without delay, "I love you too Neala." Then he kissed her tenderly on her lips, before they both enveloped each other in a much more passionate kiss. Lost deep in the effects of young love, they didn't notice the props being brought onto the stage in front of them, ready for the main attraction.

A few minutes later, their over exuberant kissing was interrupted by the same skinny man from outside, announcing the show was about to start, and that everyone should now take their seats. Glancing behind him, Lusam was shocked to see an almost a full tent of people now seated behind them. More than a few looking in his direction with a look of disgust on their faces, obviously due to his and Neala's prior activities. Turning around to face the front he sank a little lower in his chair, before reclaiming Neala's hand and settling in for the start of the show.

"Ladies and gentlemen. Please welcome on stage ... The amazing! ... The magnificent! ... The stupendous! ... THE GREAT ORMANDO!"

The crowd roared and clapped as a man dressed in a frilly white shirt and black trousers walked onto the stage. He was closely followed by a young woman dressed in a tight fitting tunic and leggings. The young woman was escorted to the far end of the stage, where she was attached to a large wooden board by her wrists and ankles. Then the Great Ormando returned to the other end of the stage, before removing a knife and demonstrating how sharp it was on a piece of paper.

Lusam realised what was about to happen just as the man let loose with his first throwing knife. It thudded into the board, just missing the young woman and gaining him huge applause from the crowd. Neala just laughed loudly, and the man on stage actually turned to look at her as it interrupted his next throw. Feeling so silly for making Neala come and watch something like this, he turned to Neala and said, "Sorry, I didn't know it would be … "

"It's fine. Don't worry. Let's watch this *Great Ormando*. Maybe he can teach me something," Neala replied, still giggling at Lusam's expense.

"Would the young lady in the front row care to share with the rest of us what she finds so amusing? Or maybe she thinks the unmatched skill of The Great Ormando is something to laugh at. If you wish to steal the attention of The Great Ormando, maybe *you* should be the one up here on stage young lady," came the sneering voice from the stage.

Lusam saw the immediate reaction in Neala's face to his challenge, and cringed at the potential outcome. "Neala … don't," was all he managed to say before she vaulted onto the stage, taking the audience and even The Great Ormando by surprise. The hushed whispers coming from the audience behind Lusam were getting louder as each person gave their prediction of what would happen next. He doubted any of them had as good an idea as he did, as to what might happen next.

The Great Ormando looked visibly shaken that Neala had responded by leaping onto the stage the way she had. He'd obviously expected a different reaction from her. Neala walked calmly over to him. She removed a knife from her belt, placed the tip of it on his chest, and walked him at least ten paces further back than where he'd thrown his earlier knife. Then she turned back towards the woman, who was now struggling frantically, without success, to free herself from her bonds. Neala removed her remaining five throwing knives, and threw one after the other, so fast that it seemed like all six were in flight at the same time. The young woman screamed and the audience's reactions ranged from gasps, to words Lusam had never even heard before. Six loud thuds confirmed all the daggers' flights had ended. Each of the six daggers were perfectly arranged to create a halo effect above the young woman's head.

The crowd was stunned into immediate silence, as each of them tried to decide if this was in fact actually part of the show. Neala casually walked over to the young woman and retrieved her knives, before whispering something to her. Jumping off the stage, she walked over to Lusam and offered him her hand, which he took as he stood up, then they left a completely silent tent behind them, and exited out into the hustle and bustle of the carnival outside. Neither Lusam or Neala noticed the two men exit the tent behind them.

Lusam waited until he thought Neala had calmed down enough. He was about to apologise for taking her to see something that she obviously would never have enjoyed, when she said, "Sorry Lusam, I didn't mean to spoil the show for you. He just really annoyed me."

"Oh, don't apologise. It was my fault for taking you to a show like that. I'm the one who should be saying sorry, not you. Besides, now he has to change his name."

Neala looked rather confused, and asked, "What do you mean, change his name?"

"Well. He can hardly claim to be *The Great Ormando, unmatched in skill* any longer can he?" Lusam replied, trying very hard to keep a straight face.

"No, I guess he can't," agreed Neala, laughing at Lusam's joke. "Come on, let's go get something to eat, then we can find a show to watch that we can both enjoy," Neala suggested.

"Okay, but only if you promise me not to throw any more of your knives at the people on stage," teased Lusam.

"That depends how bad the show is," Neala replied, grinning back at him. Both laughing, they headed off to buy something to eat.

They eventually bought some sweet pastries and other items to eat from one of the food vendors, and then made their way towards the main stage area. The man who sold them the food had informed them that the main attraction would be starting on stage in the next few minutes. He'd suggested they should try and get a good vantage point to see the show, as it was a truly excellent spectacle. Having heard similar claims from the skinny man outside the knife throwing tent, Lusam was a little sceptical about how good it would *actually* be. He decided to ask the man what kind of show it was this time, and was amazed to hear it would be a magic show.

Apart from his grandmother, Lusam had never seen anyone else do any kind of magic before. He was very interested to see what this man or woman would do on stage. He was also very surprised that anyone would openly display their ability to use magic in public; even advertising the fact.

Maybe his grandmother had been wrong after all. Maybe letting others know he could use magic wouldn't be as bad as she had thought it would be. After all, how dangerous could it be if this person was about to perform magic on a stage in front of all these people?

They both tried to make their way towards the

front of the crowd, but there were just too many people in front of them, all waiting for the main attraction to start. They decided to stay where they were, which left around twenty rows of people in front of them. The view from here was not ideal, but it was a lot better than where they had started, which was at least twice as far back.

It seemed like a long time later when a strange looking man wearing a black cloak, covered in white stars and half-moons walked onto the stage. The audience applauded loudly as he came to the centre of the stage and bowed deeply to them.

"Ladies and gentlemen. What you are about to witness is magic in its purest form. No trickery or slight of hand, only magic. Please, enjoy the show," the man announced, before taking another bow to the audience. The audience applauded loudly again, even Lusam became excited at the prospect of seeing another person perform magic, and clapped his hands enthusiastically.

Lusam instinctively slipped into his mage-sight to take a look at how bright this man's aura might be, but he was stunned to see that his aura was no brighter than most other people's in the audience. He knew this man could not possibly perform any kind of magic. In fact, he would be very surprised if he was capable of even sensing magic in others. Lusam was about to tell Neala that he was a fraud, when something else caught his attention. Right at the front of the crowd, next to the stage, was the unmistakable crimson aura of the man they'd seen several months earlier in the west district: the one who had been inspecting the bodies they had left there. A shiver ran through Lusam when he remembered the feeling this man had caused, as he probed his mind that day.

Lusam leant close to Neala and whispered, "Look, down near the front on the right. It's that man in the black robes we saw in the west district a few months ago." Neala scanned the front of the stage and nodded her agreement.

"Creepy looking guy. Maybe he's part of the carnival?"

"No, I don't think so. I never got around to telling you everything I sensed that night. Now is not the time either, but trust me, he's more than he seems," Lusam whispered in her ear. "One other thing, that guy on stage is a fraud too. He has no real magic." Neala was about to ask him if he was certain, then decided, of course, he was the best one to determine whether this man was a fraud or not, and instead said, "Oh well, at least we didn't pay for this one."

Lusam laughed in agreement with her, and they both settled in to watch the show. Neala seemed quite impressed with the various magic tricks the man performed on stage, and Lusam was sure that he would have been too, except he couldn't help himself, and kept using his mage-sight to see how the man was cheating. He had to admit, some tricks were very cleverly done, but he couldn't help feeling the man was cheating the whole audience.

When the show ended the audience roared their approval, and several young men and woman circulated throughout the crowds collecting donations for the show. Lusam was lost deep in thought, when he was abruptly brought back to reality by Neala jabbing him in the ribs. She leant towards him as if she was about to kiss his cheek, and whispered in his ear, "Don't look now, but that strange man at the front just made eye contact with me, and he's now trying to make his way towards us. I think we should leave … right now."

"Are you sure?" Lusam asked, desperately not wanting to look in the direction of the man.

"Yes, I'm sure. But, if you want to wait here to make certain and debate it …"

"No, let's go. Now!" Lusam replied shakily. He had no idea why this man made him feel the way he did. Suddenly he felt that strange feeling again, as if someone was trying to get inside his head. This time Lusam easily kept the probing of the man at bay, even though he could feel the man's strenuous efforts to try and break down his barriers. Lusam felt much less threatened by the man's power this time, but he still didn't want to wait around to meet him face to face.

They made their way through the main crowd towards the back of the town square, but it was slow progress. Once they had left the main mass of people behind, and entered the general flow of people coming and going to the carnival, Neala chanced a quick glance behind her to see if the man was still in pursuit, and was not surprised to see that he still was.

"Quickly, follow me, into that shop over there," Neala said, indicating a shop with its door wide open. As they entered, Lusam saw it was a shop selling cloth of all colours and designs. Racks and racks of cloth that formed narrow walkways between them, almost like a multicoloured maze.

Neala grabbed Lusam's hand and pulled him along behind her. She seemed to know exactly where she was going, so Lusam just followed the best he could. A few seconds later they found themselves exiting the shop through a back entrance, and onto the street behind. Neala then led him down the cobbled street and into yet another shop, this time selling flowers and cakes. Again she led him back outside through a rear door into yet another street. They repeated this another three times, each time entering by one door and leaving by another.

Lusam had no idea where they were when they

finally stopped running, and Neala pulled him inside yet another shop.

"I think we might have lost him," Neala said, glancing out of the shop window from behind a clothes rack.

Lusam was still panting for breath, but managed to ask,"How did you know which of those shops had rear doors like that?"

"It's what I do," was all she said in reply, still watching diligently for any sign of the man in black robes. They stayed in the shop for several minutes, before deciding it was time to leave and head back to the safety of *The Old Ink Well.*

Leaving the shop and gaining their bearings, they set off down the cobbled street in the direction of home, with Lusam leading the way. At the first intersection they took a left turn down another quiet cobbled backstreet. Neala suggested staying within the less busy back streets where possible, to avoid being spotted by the strange man again, and Lusam was more than happy to agree with her.

Turning the next corner Lusam was about to say

something to Neala, when he collided with someone coming around the corner from the opposite direction. Pain exploded in Lusam's stomach, and his knees buckled under him. His hands clutched at the area where the pain had erupted, and he was shocked to feel something hard protruding from his abdomen. Looking down, he saw his shirt soaked with blood, and the handle of a dagger sticking out. Gasping through the pain, he looked up at Neala with a question on his lips, but was unable to voice anything through the incredible pain. Neala screamed his name, then suddenly became a blur in front of his eyes as her daggers intercepted the man who had injured him.

Lusam found himself sitting down, leaning against the building, still clutching at the dagger in his stomach, while watching the deadly dance of Neala and the man unfold before him. It was then he noticed a second man only a few footsteps behind. He reached into his shirt to remove a throwing knife.

"LOOK OUT!" Lusam managed to shout, just in time to warn Neala of the knife flying in her direction. He wasn't sure, but it looked like Neala had already spotted the danger and reacted in time to avoid the deadly projectile.

Lusam wanted to blast the man with magic, but he was unable to concentrate enough through the pain in his gut to manage it. He knew he had to get the knife out of his stomach, then try to heal himself, so he could help Neala. And quickly.

Neala seemed to easily defend herself against the attacks of the man, and was now beginning to press her own advantage. A few seconds later the man seemed to realise he was losing the battle too, and changed his tactics to defend more than attack. Neala easily stepped past his guard, scoring minor hits, time and again, on various parts of the man's body. During one of her attacks, Lusam noticed her remove one of her throwing knives whilst she spun, releasing it a heartbeat later in the direction of the man. The knife thudded into his chest, and his eyes suddenly went wide. He instantly dropped his own dagger onto the ground with a clatter, and grasped at the handle of the knife that was now buried to the hilt in his chest. He just stared at Neala, with a look of complete disbelief on his face. How could he have been killed by this girl? He was dead before he hit the floor.

Lusam saw Neala's attention now turn to the second man, just as he was placing some kind of pipe to his lips. Lusam clearly heard him blow down the pipe and noticed several thin darts leave the end of it, each flying through the air in the general direction of Neala. Neala tried to roll to the side and avoid the darts, but one found its mark. Pulling out the dart from her leg, Neala stood up and rushed at the man with her daggers drawn. He parried her attack, then came around for an attack of his own. Lusam was no expert in knife combat, but it was obvious that he was a match for Neala's skill, and much better than the first man she'd already dispatched.

"What's your name girl?" the man asked, looking very relaxed as Neala pressed her attacks. It looked like Neala's reactions were slowing down, as the man parried her attacks more and more easily with each passing moment.

"You don't need to know my name, for me to

kill you," she hissed back at him. The man laughed at her, as he continued to defend against her ever-slowing attacks.

"If I wanted to kill you, you'd be dead already," the man said, with an amused look on his face. "Unfortunately for you, Shiva wants to *talk* with you personally back in Stelgad, regarding the theft of one of his horses. I have strict instructions to bring you to him alive and unharmed, but I can assure you, when he's finished *talking* with you, you would have preferred a quick death here by my hand."

Neala fell to one knee, desperately swinging her blade to counter any incoming attacks, but none came. Lusam realised the dart must have been poisoned, and it was rendering Neala completely defenceless. He had to do something, and fast.

Lusam closed his eyes and concentrated on blocking the pain in his stomach using his magic. Once he had blocked the pain completely, he took a hold of the dagger with both hands and prepared to remove it. He knew the blade had done a lot of damage to his abdomen, and removing it would surely do even more. He had to be ready to start repairing the damage quickly, before he lost too much blood. Feeling extremely nauseous, he took a few rapid breaths and quickly removed the dagger. Glancing up, he could see that Neala was now completely defenceless on the floor before the man, as he continued to taunt her with verbal comments.

Doubling his efforts, Lusam focused on stopping the internal bleeding, before moving outward towards the flesh wound. When he was sure all the damage had been repaired, he braced himself, before attempting to stand. Knowing the man would likely throw another knife at him as soon as he stood up, he decided to erect a force-field around himself before moving.

After encasing himself in a force-field Lusam began to stand up. The man looked fairly relaxed, and obviously didn't expect Lusam to be any threat to him after being impaled by the dagger. As expected, he calmly removed a throwing knife and launched it at Lusam's head. The knife bounced off and clattered onto the cobbled street close to the man's feet. He looked down at his knife and then back at Lusam, before retrieving his knife and examining it more closely. "Neat trick," the man said, still looking a little confused.

"If you liked that, you're going to love this one," Lusam replied, forming a fireball in his hand twice the size of a man's head, and preparing to launch it at him. The man didn't look half as scared as he should be, and Lusam admired his nerve. As Lusam prepared to send the fireball hurtling towards the man, he suddenly sensed something behind him. Turning quickly, he came face to face with the strange man in the black robes. A heartbeat later Lusam was struck by a huge invisible force that sent him hurtling backwards into the wall behind him.

Lusam was badly winded, but he knew without question that he would have been dead without his force-field in place. As he struggled to his feet again, he was suddenly frozen in place by some kind of invisible restraint. He then started to feel the now unmistakable sensation of his mind being probed by the strange man in black robes.

Looking over to where Neala still lay on the ground, he noticed she was now no longer moving. Panicking, thinking she might be dead, he checked her aura, and was relieved to see that she was merely unconscious. The other man bent down and effortlessly lifted Neala off the ground, placing her over his right shoulder, and turned to leave. Lusam tried to shout her name, but nothing came out of his mouth. It seemed he had been robbed of his speech, as well as his ability to move.

Lusam felt the strange man increase the pressure on his mind, but he still was unable to break through Lusam's defences. Lusam instinctively fell into his mage-sight to take a look at the man. He could clearly see magic being used by the man, and also noticed that there were now two layers of force-fields surrounding him. The inner one being his, and the outer one created by the strange man in the black robes. He could no longer see Neala, or the man who had taken her. He knew he had to get away from this man and rescue her; before they got too far ahead of him. Lusam had overheard the man talking to Neala, telling her that someone in Stelgad called Shiva wanted to talk with her, about the horse she had stolen. It didn't take Lusam long to work out that this *"Shiva,"* must be the boss of the rival thieves' guild that had wiped out Neala's old guild. He also guessed by the word *"talk,"* he actually meant torture, or worse.

There was no way Lusam was about to let that happen. He loved Neala with all his heart, and just the thought of anyone hurting her turned him to rage. He channelled a huge pulse of power into his own force-field, expanding it so rapidly and explosively, it shattered the force-field of the other mage. He saw the look of utter bewilderment on the face of the other mage, as he hit the floor hard with the force of the blast. The mage quickly began to stand up again, whilst chanting something over and over to himself. Lusam noticed the strange looking object forming in the right hand of the mage, as he once again stood before him.

Strengthening his own shield against whatever was about to come, Lusam braced himself. When the magical missile hit his shield it jolted him backwards, but little more. The other mage looked completely shocked that he still remained standing in front of him. He quickly sent several more of the magical missiles towards Lusam, each one impacting harmlessly on his shield. Lusam tried to speak again, but found he still couldn't make a sound. Lusam had no idea how the mage had created the spell to silence him, and he didn't know how to counteract it either.

Lusam knew he had to go after Neala right now, or it would be too late—if it wasn't already too late. Once again the restraining force-field appeared around him, but this time it was much stronger. Lusam's anger flared at what was happening to him, and his inability to rescue the one he loved, all because of this man in front of him.

Lusam channelled so much power into his own force-field it made him dizzy with the effort. As he was about to release the spell, he noticed another man turn the corner behind the mage, carrying a shield and starting to draw his sword. Lusam had had enough. He released the huge blast of power, shattering the force-field of the mage with so much force, it literally blasted the two men in front of him into the wall at the far end of the street. Instantly he knew the mage was dead, as he felt the unmistakable magical force that was released whenever a mage dies.

Lusam was about to leave and start the urgent pursuit of Neala's kidnapper, when he heard the second man stirring. The mage dying had obviously released the spell on his vocal chords, as he was able to whisper a few choice words to himself, as he watched the second man stand up at the end of the street. Not wanting to waste any more time, Lusam formed a fireball in the palm of his hand and let it loose towards the man. The man saw the incoming fireball and raised his shield to intercept the missile. When the fireball hit his shield, it simply winked out of existence with a fizzle. Lusam started to create a much larger version, but was stopped in his tracks when the man shouted,

"Lusam. Stop! I'm here to help you."

"Who are you? How do you know my name?" Lusam asked, still holding the roaring ball of fire in his right hand.

"My name is Renn, and I'm here to take you to the High Temple of Aysha in Lamuria," he said, holding his shield at the ready, just in case Lusam decided to release the missile at him.

Lusam let out a crazy sounding laugh, then replied, "I'm sorry Renn, but I'm a little busy at the moment. My best friend was just kidnapped and I have to rescue her, before they kill her."

"Wait! Your life is in great danger. This agent of Aamon is only the first of many sent to find and kill you. We must leave this place immediately. His fellow agents will have sensed his death, and will be on their way right now, as we speak. We must leave now!"

"You expect me to just trust what you say? For all I know you could have been sent here to kill me or Neala too. I'm leaving now. If you try to follow me … well, it won't be good for you," Lusam replied. Noticing Neala's throwing knife still sticking out of the first man's chest, he let the fireball fade away and went to retrieve the only thing he had left of Neala's.

"Wait, please. Look," Renn said, unbuttoning his tunic and removing a gold chain. On the gold chain was the unmistakable symbol that identified him as a Paladin of Aysha. Lusam's mind reeled at the thought that he'd just attacked a paladin of Aysha. That would explain why his fireball did no damage to his shield. It was common knowledge that weapons carried by paladins were imbued with the power of their God. Lusam said a silent prayer to Aysha, asking for forgiveness for attacking one of her paladins, before turning to Renn and apologising to him as well.

"We must leave now lad. I'll help you with your friend, but you must promise to return with me to the High Temple once we've rescued her." Lusam didn't know, or care, why Renn wanted him to go with him to the High Temple. What he did care about was getting Neala back safe, and as fast as possible.

"Okay. They have taken her to Stelgad, to a thieves' guild there. They intend to torture and kill her, we must hurry." It was just then that Lusam realised he had absolutely no idea how to get to

319

Stelgad, or even how far it was. "Do you know the way to Stelgad?" he asked Renn, walking swiftly in the direction he'd last seen the man taking Neala.

"Yes, I know how to get to Stelgad. It's a long way though. Maybe nine or ten days by road on horseback, it depends on the weather. But we can't go by road."

"Why not?" Lusam asked.

"The agents of Aamon will be watching all of the roads out of Helveel now that they know you're here. Their only mission is to kill you, no matter what the cost."

"We have to get Neala before they reach Stelgad, or she's dead! I have no choice but to risk the road," Lusam replied frantically.

"No! If you go by road, you'll both die. You're life is too important lad. We need you."

"It's not your decision! If you don't want to come … fine. I'll go alone," Lusam almost shouted at him.

"Okay, let's think about this logically. The man who has your friend left maybe twenty minutes ago, correct?"

"Yes. And the more time we waste talking, the further away he's getting with Neala."

"Okay, so how many horses do you have right now? Do you have supplies for a ten day journey? Then if you do manage to rescue her, what about the journey back again? Do you know your way there? If you do need me to show you the way, that would be double the amount of equipment and supplies you would need. It would take you at least a full day to acquire all the items you need. By that time the agents of Aamon would have found you easily, and your mission would have failed before it had even begun. Even if you managed to avoid the agents and acquired all the provisions you need, by the time you got them all, you would never catch up with them in time. We need to leave Helveel now," Renn said calmly.

"I can't just leave her to die! There must be another way. There just has to be," Lusam almost begged.

"There is. We can cut through the forest and intercept them before they reach Stelgad. We can gather and hunt food as we go, get water from the streams, and remain well away from the roads and out of the reach of agents. It will be hard going, and the pace we must set will be swift if we are to beat them to Stelgad, but we can do if we leave right now."

Lusam thought about his options, or lack thereof, and decided he must trust this paladin of Aysha, with both his and Neala's life. He nodded his agreement to Renn, and they both set off quickly in the direction of the forest and Stelgad beyond.

Chapter Eleven

Skelly had no idea who the strange man in the black robes had been, or how the boy had managed to thwart his throwing knife as he did. If he didn't know better, Skelly would have sworn the boy's wound had healed itself, by the way he seemed to move without the encumbrance of pain when he stood up and moved towards him.

Too many strange and unexplained events to risk getting involved in someone else's fight, Skelly thought. He'd also experienced a strange feeling in his mind as he looked at the man in the black robes, as if he was crawling through his head, looking for something.

Skelly wasn't often afraid of anything, least of all an unarmed boy and a strange looking man in a robe with no apparent weapons. This time however, his instincts screamed at him to get out of there, fast. If there was one thing in this life he was sure of, it was to trust his instincts. They had saved his hide more times than he cared to mention. And he wasn't about to start ignoring them now.

Carrying the unconscious girl over his shoulder, he quickly made his way back to the horses. Carter had been a good fighter, but he wouldn't be hard to replace by the guild, so he wouldn't be missed much either. One advantage of his demise was that Skelly now had a spare horse to carry the girl, instead of having to double up on one horse. *It would certainly make for a faster and more comfortable trip back to Stelgad, and that alone was worth losing Carter for,* Skelly thought, allowing himself a wry smile.

Reaching the abandoned warehouse where they had left the horses and supplies, it didn't take him long to saddle them and prepare to leave Helveel. He lay, the still unconscious girl across the saddle, and fastened her on securely with a rope so she wouldn't fall off, or try to escape when she woke up. He removed a bottle of whisky from one of the saddlebags and poured some onto the girl's face and hair, then took a swig for himself, before returning the bottle to the saddlebag. He knew the poison would probably render her unconscious for another couple of hours at least. He did have an antidote with him, but decided it would be easier to leave town with her in this condition, rather than her screaming or trying to fight him from the saddle of her horse.

When they reached the town gates two guards saw their approach and stepped out to stop them in their tracks.

"Halt!" one of the guards said loudly, holding up his hand.

Stopping several paces away, Skelly replied, "Good afternoon gentlemen. How may I be of service?"

"What's the meaning of this? What business do you have with that girl there?" the other guard asked, nodding towards the girl tied onto the saddle face down.

"Oh, don't worry about her gentlemen. She's just my wayward niece. She came to the carnival to have a good time, but I'm afraid her and her friends had a little *too* much of a good time this afternoon. I caught her with an almost empty bottle of whisky, slumped in the corner of the town square. I didn't want her causing you good fellows any trouble, so I decided to take her home for her father to deal with her—when she finally wakes up, that is. Although, I think her headache will be punishment enough," Skelly replied laughing loudly.

The first guard approached the girl and lifted her head with a suspicious look on his face. He leant close to her mouth and sniffed, pulling back swiftly at the stench of alcohol radiating from her. He turned to his comrade in arms and nodded. The second guard briefly looked back at Skelly, before waving him on through the gates.

"Make sure she doesn't make a habit of it in the future," he said, as they past through the gates.

"Oh, I can absolutely guarantee she won't give

you any trouble in the future gentlemen," Skelly replied, grinning at the guard, then looking at the girl tied to the saddle.

It was almost three hours later, when they were well out of sight of Helveel, that Neala began to stir. Her head spun, and her vision was blurry. Her ribs were on fire, and it was hard to catch her breath as she was being jolted continuously. When Neala could finally focus her vision, she recognised that she was looking at the ground as it continuously flashed by at a constant speed. She could see the legs of a horse. A horse she was riding. No. Not riding. Trying hard to get her mind to work, and thinking through the haze that was clouding her thoughts, she realised she was somehow tied to the horse.

Neala remained silent for several minutes, trying to make sense of her situation. She could see the man she had fought in front of her on another horse, but she wasn't sure if anyone was following behind without turning her head to see. But that would let anyone who might be there know she was awake, and that would negate her small advantage. She listened carefully for the sound of hooves behind her, but heard none. She needed to know what she was up against, so she decided to turn her head and look to be sure. As she suspected, it was just her and this one man. Returning to her original position, she closed her eyes again and tried to think of a way out of the situation she now found herself in.

It was about another hour before the horses stopped and she heard the man dismount, then start walking towards her. Still feigning unconsciousness, she lay motionless and waited.

"There's no point pretending to be asleep still. I know you're not. The poison I gave you doesn't last that long," he said, circling her horse and coming to stand in front of her face. Neala remained silent and didn't move. "You have two choices: you can ignore me and stay tied to that saddle until we reach Stelgad, or you can talk to me and ride upright. Your choice. It doesn't bother me either way," the man said, waiting for an answer. Neala knew she couldn't remain here much longer without doing some serious damage to herself, so she relented and answered the man.

"Who are you? And what do you want with me?" she spat at him. The man laughed at her, then slapped her hard across the face, making her wince, and her eyes water.

"Who I am, is the person taking you back to Stelgad to face justice for your crimes. The only thing I want from you is a little respect, and some peace and quiet during the trip back. Now … here's how this will work. If you co-operate, I'll secure you in an upright position, instead of how you are now. I'm sure it would be much more comfortable for you.

"Unfortunately, I have strict instructions to deliver you to Stelgad alive. That doesn't mean I can't cut you up plenty on the way there though. If you try to escape, I'll make sure walking is not an option for you, ever again. If you give me any other kind of trouble, I'll simply put you back to sleep until we reach Stelgad. Do you understand my terms?"

Neala already knew she couldn't stay tied to the saddle as she was now, or she would be in very bad shape before the day was done, let alone all the way back to Stelgad. Reluctantly she decided to agree with him.

"Yes, I understand," she hissed at him. The man slapped her again, this time harder. Her ears rang with the impact, and she saw stars in her vision. She gasped at the sudden pain, but tried hard not to cry out.

"I said I required your respect. Your answer didn't sound very respectful to me. Try again," he said calmly, standing close to her down turned face.

"Yes, I understand," Neala replied again, trying to sound as genuine as possible this time.

"Good. Much better," the man said, as he cut the rope that connected her hands and feet under the horse. Neala wasn't ready for her sudden release, and found herself crashing to the floor, where she sat winded trying to catch her breath. The man bent down and lifted Neala easily off the floor by her arm, and back onto her feet.

"What's your name girl?" the man asked, still holding on to her arm. Neala couldn't see any advantage in not telling him her name. She doubted he would have heard of her before anyway.

"Neala … my name's Neala. What's yours?" As soon as she asked his name, she regretted doing so, fully expecting another painful reminder not to ask questions. The man laughed out loud at her, before replying,

"You can call me Skelly," he replied casually. Skelly then bent down and untied the rope from around one of her ankles: so her feet were no longer tied together. Neala probably would have tried to kick him in the face and flee at that point, but the name he'd just given her, made her think twice. She'd heard the name "Skelly" many times before in Stelgad. And what she knew of that name, made her quickly reassess her situation. If this was the same Skelly as the one she'd heard of, she was in even bigger trouble than she thought. His reputation as a cold-hearted killer, unequalled with a blade did nothing to put her at ease. She had no doubt he would carry out his threats if she gave him even the slightest cause to do so.

Her mind turned to Lusam at that point.

Instantly, she felt guilty of not thinking of him sooner. She needed to find out what had happened to him, but she knew questioning Skelly directly, would likely earn her only more pain. She decided to try and use a different tactic instead.

Smiling at him, she replied, "Pleased to meet you Skelly." He looked at her with cold blue eyes, trying to spot any sarcasm in her face, but saw none. Neala could see the unasked question on his face, and decided to be bold enough to answer it for him. "I figured if we'll be travelling together for more than a week, we might as well be civilised with each other," she said, still smiling. He looked at her for a moment longer, then just nodded his agreement.

"Get back on your horse, we have a long way to travel today," he said, taking hold of the horses reigns. She did as he asked, and he retied her feet under the belly of her horse, and her hands to the saddle.

"May I ask you something before we set off please," Neala asked hopefully.

"You can ask," he replied, tying Neala's horse

to his saddle.

"Did you kill the boy I was with?" she asked, trying not to choke on the words. Skelly turned in his saddle to look at her, obviously contemplating whether to answer her question or not.

"No, I didn't kill him. The knife that my associate put in his belly probably did though. The last I saw of him, he was having problems of his own with some guy in black robes. Neither your boyfriend or the man in robes are any of my concern, so I have no idea what became of either of them." He turned his back to Neala and kicked his horse into movement without another word. It was a good job Neala's hands were tied to the saddle as her horse jolted into motion, or she would have found herself on the ground again.

Her mind was reeling at the information Skelly had just shared with her. She didn't think he would lie to her about not killing Lusam. *That wasn't his style,* she thought. She knew nothing about the man in black robes, other than he had tried to pursue them in Helveel. She knew some of what Lusam was capable of with his magic, and felt confident he would have protected himself against the man in the black robes. She thought about the knife in his belly, and knew he was capable of healing that injury too, given enough time. That was the problem, had Lusam had enough time to heal himself before confronting the man in black robes? She just had no way to know. For the rest of the afternoon she remained silent, constantly playing out the possibilities in her mind over and over. She knew if Lusam *was* still alive, he would be coming to try and save her. All she could do now was wait and hope he would come.

As they approached a fork in the road, Neala became aware of two men stood in the road blocking their path. Neala took a sharp intake of breath, as she noticed them both wearing black robes, identical to the man's in Helveel. Skelly didn't slow the horses as he approached the men, but Neala noticed him visibly tense up when the two men made eye contact with him. Shortly afterwards, they focused their attention on Neala, and she too involuntarily tensed up, as she felt a strange sensation wash over her. It was like thousands of ants crawling around in her head, then it stopped just as suddenly as it had started. The two men moved to the side of the road, and let them pass unchallenged.

It was at least a mile further down the road before Neala felt confident enough to speak. "You felt that too, right?" she asked.

"I did," Skelly replied, without turning his head, or slowing his horse. Neala offered a silent prayer to Aysha that Lusam would survive and find her in time, then resigned herself to her fate if he didn't.

Acknowledgements

It is my sincere hope that you enjoyed reading this book as much as I enjoyed writing it, and I hope you will join Lusam and Neala again as their quest continues in The Dragon-Mage Wars series, Book two. I would like to take this opportunity to thank all the people who offered me support and encouragement during the long days, and weeks writing this series of books. I would especially like to thank my wife, without whom I'm sure this project would never have seen the light of day, and my two boys Luke and Sam, who were obviously my inspiration for the main character Lusam. The biggest thank you goes to you, the reader, without whom none of this would be worthwhile.

mail@deancadman.com
www.deancadman.com

Please email me if you wish to be added to my book mailing list, you will receive updates on forthcoming books and release dates, plus much more. First edition signed copies of this book are also available while stocks last.